THE BUTTERFLY TREE:
AN ANTHOLOGY OF BLACK WRITING
FROM THE UPPER MIDWEST

THE BUTTERFLY TREE

AN ANTHOLOGY OF BLACK WRITING FROM THE UPPER MIDWEST

Edited by
Conrad Balfour

Graphics by
Ta-coumba T. Aiken
and
Seitu Jones

Many Minnesotas Project #2
New Rivers Press
1985

The Butterfly Tree has been published with the aid of grant support from the Northwest Area Foundation, the First Bank System Foundation, the Norwest Bank Corporation, the Arts Development Fund of the United Arts Council, and the McKnight Foundation.

New Rivers Press books are distributed by

Bookslinger	and	Small Press Distribution
213 East 4th St.		1784 Shattuck Ave.
St. Paul, MN		Berkeley, CA
55101		94709

The Butterfly Tree has been manufactured in the United States of America for New Rivers Press (C. W. Truesdale, editor/publisher), 1602 Selby Ave., St. Paul, MN 55104 in a first edition of 1,500 copies.

PUBLISHER'S NOTE

The Butterfly Tree, edited by novelist Conrad Balfour, is the second in an on-going series of ethnic anthologies published by New Rivers Press as part of its *Many Minnesotas Project*. We hope, in time, to present to the reading public a comprehensive collection of regional writing that truly represents the multifarious heritages making up the background of the population of this part of America. Most of the writing in these anthologies is by living Americans, some of whom have gained professional recognition for their work but many of whom have never been published before. ("Whistling Woman," for instance, the story by Soyini Guyton which appears in *The Butterfly Tree*, is her first published work.)

The reader will find a broad range of material here, in poetry and prose, and, even more significantly, a great variety in style, voice, and subject matter. Certainly the "Black experience" is reflected in many ways — the sense of alienation or alternative ways of perceiving reality, and the inevitable rebelliousness of the young and the not-so-young, which is so dramatically reflected in Pamela Fletcher's story, "The Parting." But what is most striking to the non-Black reader (including this one) is the sense of craft and the desire to excel, radiating throughout this collection. The nostalgia for a way of life closer to nature and the land, a nostalgia common to most urbanites, is present here as might be expected, but it comes out in sometimes utterly unique and beautiful ways, as in Alexs D. Pate's story "The Butterfly Tree." Equally apparent in this material is the desire for a reconciliation that transcends race and is truly visionary. Nowhere is this spirit better reflected than in the graphics by Ta-coumba T. Aiken, most of which were done especially for this collection.

— C. W. Truesdale
St. Paul, Minnesota
December 1985

THE BUTTERFLY TREE

Graphics

Ta-coumba T. Aiken, *front cover, pages 10, 36, 44, 54, 85, 86, 92, 117, 122, 130, 135, 142, 147, 175, and 185*

Seitu Jones: *pages 22, 40, 50, 120, 148, and 176*

THE BUTTERFLY TREE

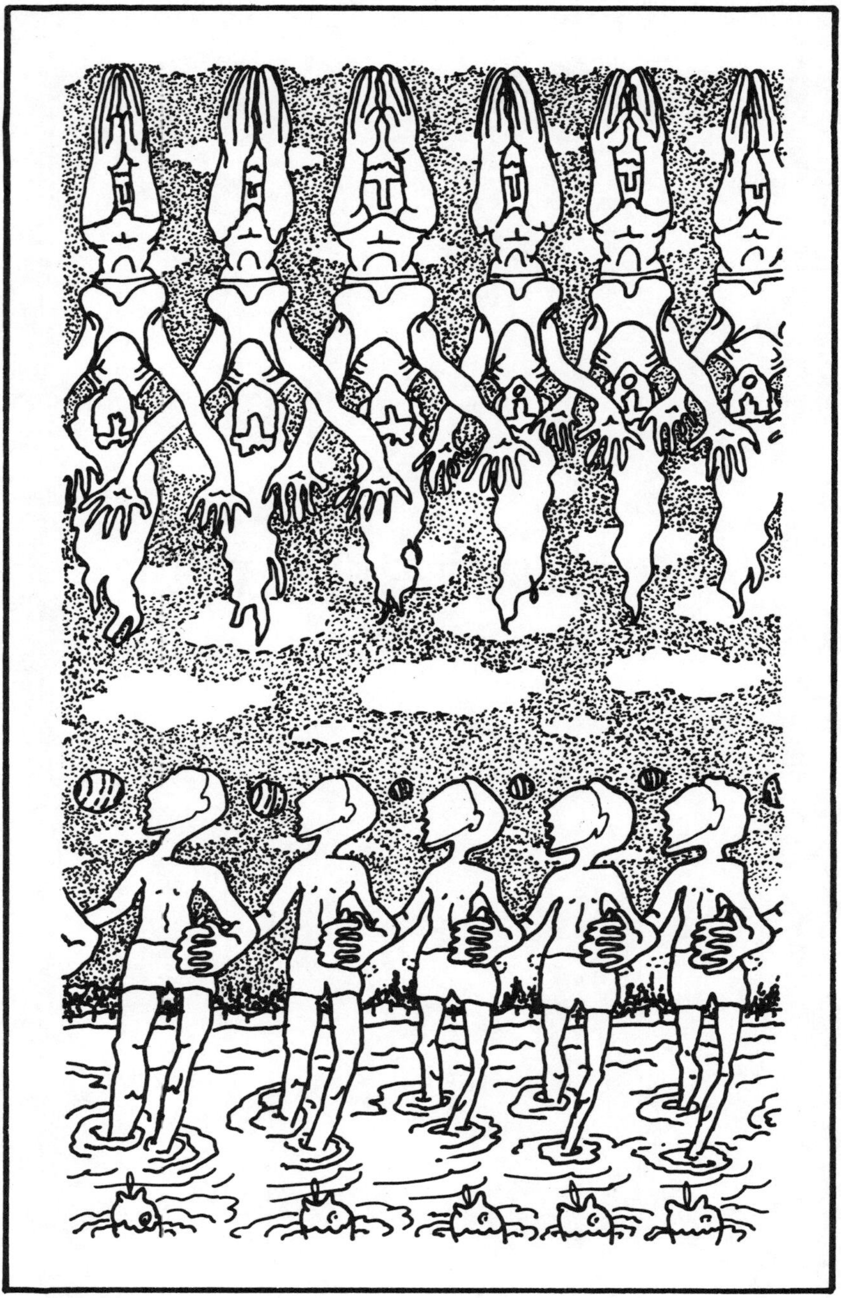

TRAVELLER'S RETURN

Marcella Taylor

The gypsy whispers,
her voice still shrill,
It is a bad time
for travelling, many losses.

But I have sold it all, the bits
of bent and scratched kitchenware,
soiled mattresses, clothing that refuses
to envelop the swelling body,

the clock whose alarm never stops,
the vacuum that collects only surface dirt,
the television, bent antenna
receiving only faraway messages,

the turntable with its steady drone,
the heat-kissed guitar turned tone-clear
under the spell of a new mistress,
the trunk with no bounty left to store.

We scramble into the terminal, lightly
brushing away the threat of tears
behind a windshield. I drag along
bags bearing scanty pieces of clothing,

paper stacking words that duskily echo
the lost debris. I smile only
at my nephew's bronzed cheeks. He stands
protected by luggage

having held all objects beyond reach
of the buyers, returning home laden
with an array of rainbow-colored parchments,
plastic and textile memories. On the flight

south, he sings of summer. Disembarking,
his rosy-cheeked puppet turns
to the pilot. In his high-pitched
voice, he says, Goodbye America.

SHEDDING THEIR SKINS

Marcella Taylor

They burn their bodies brown
the inhabitants of this flesh
that took a skyscraper
winter to brighten

After the visitation of dark
continents, they are obsessed
assume darker tones
with each new splash in brooks
that grow beside the freeway
with each fresh stretch
among grasses
hiding their naked backs

These children of the city
work each summer
to turn the sunspots
into one smooth stain
They would become new peoples

MOVING INTO SPACE

For Juan

Marcella Taylor

He is a little boy
from a southern land, eyes filled
with the expectancy
of mounting snow, heart filled
with the sun of summer.

He seeks playmates, struggles
to share the excitement of seeing
a museum mummy, excelling
at reading, touching a chest
centuries old, discovering
one new light in the galaxy.

The boys with hair not quite blond,
their nordic-german bodies, their more
deliberate gaits, turn away to talk
of visits to their grandmothers,
visits to their uncles,
visits to their second cousins.

He cares and does not care.
His love for smiling faces goes back
to toddling time, his pain
for eyes turning toward a shapeless wall
keeps pace. He hoards
his life of spaceships, multiple moons,

old traintracks, occult visions,
living pyramids. He spends his days
imitating a monkey having a breakdown,
figuring out new inventions,
each fresh morning looking out
with love for evidence of snow.

Like the winter
his time will come
filled with the search
for January stars.

VISTA IN JOLIET

Marcella Taylor

Down by a strange dirt-filled shore
elders from old world countries
fill their gardens with virgin shrines
lit by red petals.
The houses
all look toward the water
hidden from view
by trees that breathe contaminated air.
A few streets away the dark faces of the new world
loiter on sidewalks marked with lines
of unpacked cartons. They shade their eyes
to see beyond the faded brick
that blocks their view.

A WALK ON DIVISION STREET

Marcella Taylor

The water hides behind buildings,
emerges only at five corners.
Behind railings, it sings
to morning walkers, whispers
answers to the secret air.

The bank is dressed in weekend
nudity. The jeweler has taken
a coffee break. His assistant
with the one-eyed glass
smiles at my disintegrating frames.

He mumbles of nuts
and threading. I stand
at a half-angle moving into
blindness, fingering figures
back into existence.

Down the block, I pass over
exposed cartridges, reflections
of unrecalled movements, caring
but slightly which gestures
are captured, which lost.

Neutral stills
now speak louder
moments held and passed
redeemed acts frozen
silhouetted into being
In the bookstore, I flit
from Jung to Lessing, shuffle pages
of Mother Earth, seek for the right binder
to hold fleeting minutes
find nothing, possess nothing.

The way home gradually slopes, leaves
the river no glances, no regrets.
The day is the last of Indian summer
surviving itself. Tomorrow, thawed ice
will seep beneath the floor mats

Winter will struggle to seal out
the dew. We will delay moving
the door back on its hinges,
try to capture these days, these
streets, these moments of stasis
these black and white dreams.

ISLAND WOMAN

Marcella Taylor

Your wedding picture hangs in state
in the livingroom of these middle years.
The groom's striped waistcoat covers
his hips, your bridal train stretches
white beneath the thick leaves
of the southern reaches of the Atlantic.

Eyes turned toward each other
you do not see
a grandchild disturb the floating
goldfish of an indoor aquarium.

You were born here,
married here, began days as wife
in small stone dwellings built
by an older generation, used outhouses,
oillamps to sew by
as the island darkened
to become one with the sea.

Unlike others, you laid aside
the urge to pack heavy brown luggage,
explore lands swiftly losing
their boasted treasures. You knew
that much too soon these modest
hills, gray rocks, turquoise waters
would stumble into the drier world.

Now you lead the village band,
reconcile the island's accounts,
preside over seven carpeted rooms,
manage houses for absent owners.
How often do you escape to ramble still
isolated and thickly-wooded hills,

skirting the stones with the skill
of youth, cast eyes toward the miles
of dark waters

a magic serpent commissioned
to girdle borders of your elected world.

MARIJUANA CATCH

Marcella Taylor

A woman of the island
strolled on a still Sunday
afternoon in a temperate garden.

Palms and other rich green flora,
ordered and abundant, greeted her
on either side of a path cleared

to meet the waters. The winds
that coiled around the garden
mitigated the perfume of the sun's

bath, hinted at the earthy odor
of the forbidden grass
burnt by her husband

on an isolated stretch of sand
to the north
by strict order of the chief.

DRIVING TO ESCAPE THE STORM

Marcella Taylor

We drove out from the city toward the hills
that hold firm like family jewels
leaving behind—we thought—
the threat of hurricane Belle
I hardly noticed the receding of the eaves
of those buildings I love
   or where the river went
   not because of you
   but because of the hills

Making good time, we established
my method of constructing poems
the contents of your rhetoric text
the egos poised to welcome us
you referred to your friend
professor like yourself commuting by train
to a city down the coast
do you take her for granted
both of you, tentative, middle-aged
a youthful look, property of a life
of part-time responsibilities

I, too, am a part of that
  the instability
  the struggle with expressiveness
but I have a strange passion
for that coastal city now at our backs
the advancing hills, the freeway
I hate myself, this love that travels less
towards those that hold these lands in trust

The wind, the rains were so close
but your quiet unconcern about life
your insouciance against the battles
made our voices wry, sentences farcical

Never, I know, can you adapt
to your flowing narratives
my way of using a fresh page
for the slightest revision
I am concerned with heirlooms
that reach me only as debt

I try to connect with this envy
of your compatibility
your tenuous hold on the world
like this summer
      both of us writing among hills
       that slightly tower over singing brooks

Your detachment scrapes me
here below the skin
where I shake off invasion
it would have been better
to postpone the journey
stay in the city
wait out the storm—still
not being able to read the difference
between healing and destruction
retreat is the only viable act

and if we had stayed

if we had
we would have settled in
for one more night
      you in your river drive apartment
      calling your friend to pass the time
      me a reluctant guest
      in a row of family brownstones
      on the edge of the inner city
      waiting for the winds
      that anyway
      decided to go
      where we hadn't

BITS OF NATURE

Marcella Taylor

Walking these sandy beaches,
we cannot escape attack.
Small brown particles fasten
our clothing into bundles.
The soles of our feet
and the palm of our hand
are pierced by slivers of wood.

Even if we begin
to wear shoes
our bodies
will enclose souvenirs
of daytime dreams.

We move our eyes
over a horizon thick with color,
praying that we may be blessed
to carry these shapes
toward plains far from the sea.

These winds
that twist our garments
will reach the mainland
drained too soon
of the smell of salt.

We must be ambassadors
deputized to preserve
the residue
of this land secure
beneath our skins.

THE PARTING

Pamela R. Fletcher

It was eight o'clock in the morning when the phone rang. I should have answered it. I listened from my bed while Aunt Trina, standing in the hall near my bedroom door, cooed into the phone.

"Hi, sugar. I'm just fine. No, of course not. You know I get up with the roosters around here," she said.

"No, Jessalyn's still in bed. Don't worry about that lazy child," she continued, her tone hardening. "She needs to get up anyway. Yes . . . I see . . . Oh, how nice of you to offer. Bless your heart." Her voice softened again.

"But no thank-you. I should ride with Jessalyn so you can concentrate on getting the party together. No, no no, Teddy. You heard what I said now. You must respect your elders, young man," she laughed, sounding like a giggly little girl.

"Yes, I suspect she'll have the decency to show up. After all, it is her son's birthday." Aunt Trina now spoke loudly for my benefit.

"I told you that I'm going tomorrow," I yelled. "Why wouldn't I?"

"Why would you care?" she yelled back.

"What?" I said, getting up. "Why do you insist on—" Oh hell, I thought. Why bother?

I walked out of the bedroom, passing Aunt Trina in the hall. She turned her back to me and picked up the base of the phone. She cradled it as if to guard it. My face must have conveyed the urge to grab it and slam down the receiver.

When I got to the bathroom door, I turned to look at her. She was now whispering and looking at me with the same disdain she wore when she opened the door and found me standing on the porch with my luggage one year ago.

"Where the babies? And where is your husband?" she said.

"I need to come home for a while, Aunt Trina."

She looked as if she wanted to spit on me.

"You lunatic. There's something unnatural about a woman who runs out on her babies."

Aunt Trina didn't ask why or how long. She just limped into her sewing room and closed the door.

I stood on the porch, looking at Effania, the old cat that had been around since Uncle Clarence died seven years ago.

"Where have you been, Jessi?" Her gray eyes seemed to say.

"Effania, I'm not that bad, am I?" I said, stooping over to rub her head.

But with the cool indifference of a feline, she turned away, leaving me with a yearning to bulldoze Aunt Trina's sewing room.

"Goddamn it, Katrina," I wanted to shout like I had often heard Uncle Clarence shout. "Come out of that blasted room and fight."

23

Instead I went to the guest room and unloaded my thing. I eventually went to sleep.

I didn't see her until dinner time that evening. Her almond-shaped eyes were like slits in her small, oval face.

Two days had passed before she actually paid any attention to me. On the evening of the second day, I sat outside her locked sewing room, hugging my knees, rocking back and forth, and sobbing. I wanted her to rush out and hold me like she did that time when Anthony Tilford slapped me and called me a "saddity bitch" in front of the whole track team because I refused to go with him to the Christmas Ball.

But she acted as if she wasn't on the other side of that door. I could hear her humming, "Oh Mary Don't You Weep."

I banged on the door.

"Aunt Trina, I want to talk to you. Please."

She just hummed louder. I thought I'd never forgive her.

Sometime during the night I fell asleep while sitting on the couch. Aunt Trina came out of her sewing room, removed my shoes and laid me down gently. She covered me with the quilt she had just finished making. Half asleep, I reached around her neck and she hugged me. Yet, the next morning she ignored me as she had days before.

A week later, one Saturday morning, Aunt Trina finally began to speak to me. We were sitting at the kitchen table. I had just finished making hash browns with Italian sausage and buttermilk biscuits, her favorite breakfast.

Instead of saying her usual, "Thank-you, sugar; you're so thoughtful," she said as she poured a cup of coffee:

"I am so ashamed, Jessalyn. Everybody saw you come back and they want to know what's going on. 'Is your niece visiting for a few days?' and 'How's Jessi enjoying her vacation?' and 'Her husband must be real sweet to let her come alone.' Now, they all know that you just live on the other side of town. They know something's wrong. What am I supposed to say?"

"Tell them that it's none of their business. And, besides, that busybody Elly Johnson—"

"Mrs. Johnson," she said, looking at me with a "I raised you better than that" scowl.

"Whatever. She's the only one who saw me. I'm not worried about these nosey people around here."

"Well, you ought to be."

"Well, I'm not, Aunt Trina."

"You're the talk of the neighborhood."

"Good," I said, smiling. "They need some excitement around here, anyway."

"I don't believe you, child. Your attitude and behavior is scandalous."

"That's an Elly Johnson quote if I've ever heard one," I laughed.

"You know," I continued, trying to sound serious, "I think I'll just go over and have a talk with Mrs. Johnson. I may as well tell her myself. What can you tell *her? You don't know what's happening—"*

"You're a lunatic, that's why."

"Well tell her that," I said. I got up and set my full plate on the stove.

"Enjoy your breakfast," I added, leaving the kitchen and walking out of the front door. I knew she hated to eat alone.

Prior to that week, our relationship was decent and sometimes it was even good. Although Aunt Trina was set in her ways, causing us to argue as mothers and daughters often do, warmth and affection existed between us. As I grew up, she provided me with every opportunity she had and didn't have during her childhood.

When I was ten, she sent me to charm school where I learned how to walk with good posture, how to set a table and how to eat soup properly.

She taught me how to sew and crochet (things I hated to do), corrected my English all day long, insisted that I do homework every evening even when I had none (she'd create some), and sent me to Spellman College.

Aunt Trina made certain that I associated with 'wholesome' young people and dated young men with potential.

She was typical: She didn't seem any different from any of my friends' mothers, except she was my aunt, my mother's older and only sibling. She was the only mother I knew.

And Barrydale Street, LaPuente, California was my only real home. I had no where else to go after I left Teddy and the boys. Although she and Uncle Clarence had told me that I could always come home, she didn't mean it. She was determined to make me feel as uncomfortable as possible. As far as she was concerned, I belonged in West Covina where Teddy and I settled after we got married four years ago.

Teddy wanted children right away, so nine months later I gave birth to Theodore Junior. I thought I was ready for my new adult life, but I was only playing house. A year later, I had Albert James III, named after Teddy's father and grandfather.

Albert James was born prematurely and had to stay in the hospital for several weeks. After I brought him home, I couldn't handle him. He was constantly sick and irritable, making me tired and upset. I grew weary of his incessant crying.

I felt that he didn't like me and that I was an awful mother. I couldn't bear the thought, but I didn't like my own child. Some days I came close to smothering him.

One evening I screamed at Albert James so loudly I'm sure the people in Covina Hills, fifteen miles away, could hear me.

"Jessi, calm down," Teddy said, rushing into the room. He picked up the baby, whose shrill crying turned into panting.

"You're making this child a nervous wreck, not to mention yourself," he

25

said, walking around the room and singing to the baby.

Albert James had stopped panting by then. Teddy managed to stick the formula into his mouth.

"I'm not happy here, Teddy. This is all a terrible mistake."

"Jessi, it's not uncommon for new mothers to go through this kind of depression. You just need to adjust, that's all."

"I don't want this."

"You'll be all right. Give it time. You had it easier with Theodore, but that's because he's different. He's stronger. They're different people, Jessi. Albert James is sickly but he'll grow out of it. Didn't Dr. Wells say that? He should know—"

"Teddy, I'm not ready."

"You're tired, honey, and you look it. Go to bed and get some sleep. I'll take care of him. See? He's fine now."

"You're not listening, damn it. I said I don't want it any more. I want a divorce."

Teddy stopped walking. He looked directly at me for the first time.

"I'm going to pretend that I didn't hear that, Jessalyn. You're tired and talking out of your head."

"I mean it, Teddy. I'm not crazy."

"Well, you can forget it. I don't believe in it. And another thing: this baby is your son just like Theodore is. Things get a little tough and you're ready to run, but I'm not letting you go. So, if you aren't ready now to be a mother, you better get ready."

Although I have seen Teddy at least once a month since I left, we have not talked about my returning. Every time I see him I nervously expect him to ask me when I'm coming back. But we avoid the subject and behave politely toward each other.

I suspect that he's getting advice on how to handle this situation because he's being unusually patient. I have a feeling, however, that tomorrow he will ask me if I'm ever coming back.

After dressing, I walked into the kitchen. I sat at the table with a cup of tea. Aunt Trina was standing at the counter peeling peaches for a peach cobbler.

"Aunt Trina, can I get something for you while I'm out? I'm going to the Puente Hills Mall to get the boys some things."

"You feeling guilty all of a sudden this morning?"

"What do you mean?"

"It's Theodore Junior's birthday. Why are you getting them both a gift?"

"I feel like it, that's why. What's wrong with that?"

"You think your gifts are going to compensate for your absence? You did the same thing on Albert James' birthday. Spending outlandish amounts of money on things that they will soon outgrow."

"They're my kids, Aunt Trina, I do what I want."

"Then why aren't you taking care of them? I never thought I'd see such a day. I expected better from you."

"What?"

"Why do you have to be like her? I tried my best to raise you like she should have, and you're doing the same damn thing. I thought I'd never live to witness such a thing about you. Well, you liked to have killed me. Haven't I been a good example to you, child? Lord knows I've tried with both you girls."

Aunt Trina was now mixing pie crust with flour dusted hands. Her back was turned as she stood at the counter but I could tell she was about to cry. She tapped her nervous foot, creating a monotonous rhythm.

"She left you here one morning, I mean just up and flew out of here like a bat out of hell. Without one word—"

"You told me," I said, feeling annoyed.

"I couldn't have children, so I didn't know what to do with you, Jessi—you were such a sweet little thing. And Clarence said, 'The Lord meant this child for us, Katrina,' after months had passed without any word from her.

"But I was still afraid that she'd come back and snatch you away from us. She stayed away, though, and I tried to make your life whole, to be all the mother that I could possibly be, with God's help."

"She did what she had to do," I said, trying to sound even-toned.

"She must have known that I'd be better off with you and Uncle Clarence, Aunt Trina. I know I couldn't have asked for better parents."

"You were a gift from God, even if she had no business being so grown long before she had a right to be."

Aunt Trina finally turned to look at me. She wiped her eyes, leaving flour smudges on her face.

"You were her responsibility, but we would have helped her. She knew that. What is in you all's blood that makes you run out on your own babies?"

"Shut up," I shouted. "What do you really know about us? I don't know how she felt, but I can guess. Maybe she didn't want what you wanted for her, what you thought was best for her. Like me," I said, pointing to myself.

"I've never really wanted what you wanted for me. But all my life I felt I had to do exactly what you wanted. All my life I've been trying to repay you—"

"Repay me? For what?"

"For being there for me, for being my mother. So, when you wanted me to marry Teddy because of what you felt he could offer me, being from such a 'good and respected' family, I did it for you." I said the word "you" so loudly I startled us both.

Aunt Trina wiped her hands on her embroidered apron and reached for her cane that leaned against the lower cupboard. She limped to the table and stood before me.

"I tried to do my best. I only wanted the best for you, Jessi. I thought you wanted the same things."

27

"But you never asked me what I wanted, Aunt Trina. And you're right. I also thought I wanted the same things."

"What do you want, child?"

"I don't know," I said, suddenly feeling immature and foolish.

"Then I don't know either," she said, slumping into a chair and staring into a space.

I didn't know what I wanted because all my life Aunt Trina had made my decisions for me. I would get angry and we would fuss and fight about it, but actually I preferred it that way.

It wasn't until Uncle Clarence died that I realized that Aunt Trina wouldn't be around to take care of me forever. When Teddy and I begun dating, I became so attached to him, becoming as dependent on him as I had become on Aunt Trina.

"I want to take care of you, Jessi. Please marry me," he said after we had been dating for ten months.

"Please say yes," he added when I didn't answer quickly enough for him.

"I need time to think about it, Teddy."

"Don't you love me?"

"I think so."

"I know you do. Say yes."

"Tell him yes," Aunt Trina said when I told her later.

"He's perfect—a fine young man, just like Clarence was. You let him go, every young woman this side of the Pacific will be after him. Mark my words."

We were married seven months later against my better judgment.

The next day Aunt Trina and I went to Theodore's birthday party. As soon as we walked in, Vivian, Teddy's mother, greeted us with Albert James in her arms. I took him from her and kissed him on the forehead. I put him down and then called Theodore. He ran to me with outstretched arms. We hugged and kissed each other. He led Albert James away, carrying the gifts I brought them.

"Feeling better these days, or should I say months?" Vivian said. She gave me a glass of chablis.

Aunt Trina winced at Vivian's insinuation that I was ill, even though she, herself, thought so.

"Couldn't be better, thank-you," I replied.

"So happy to hear it, m'dear," she smiled. "A little rest can do wonders, wouldn't you both agree?"

Neither I nor Aunt Trina responded. When we sat down, Vivian sat beside me.

"Now that you're feeling better, Jessalyn, have you given any thought to when you're returning?" Vivian continued.

"Yes, Jessalyn, we've all been so concerned about you," Candice, Teddy's younger sister said. She sat nearby on an armchair.

"Don't stay away too long. Your children may forget you," she added.

"I doubt that, Candice," I said. "We still keep in touch. I'm never far away."

"But, you're never *close* enough," Sandra, Teddy's older sister said as she approached us from the kitchen.

Aunt Trina looked at me. She probably sensed that I was angry by now. She shook her head slightly to indicate that I should just ignore them.

"I love your concern," I said, grinning at them. "But, it's none of your business." I rose from my seat. "By the way, nice party, wouldn't you agree?" I walked away to sit with the children.

They sat in a tight group, intently watching Teddy's father perform magic tricks.

Albert James had just gotten over a cold, but he looked well and was giggling and talking. He looked adorable. He was dressed in blue suspender short pants, a swiss dot bow tie and white knee high socks.

All the adults were watching me when I picked him up and sat him on my lap. I bounced him on my knees and sang, "London Bridge's Falling Down," a song I had often heard Teddy sing to him. He giggled and clapped, singing along. I held him closer, not once feeling apprehensive, and kissed his head, ears, neck, face and hands. He hugged and kissed me in return. Later, as I moved around the house, he was always nearby, either holding my hand or sitting on my lap.

Teddy was walking about taking picture after picture. Theodore was racing around, calling me constantly: "Look, Mommy," and "See, Mommy?" and "Come here, Mommy." I had dreaded the party all week, but now I was glad I came despite Teddy's sisters and mother.

At one point, Teddy brushed against me while we were helping Theodore open his presents. He looked at me as if he wanted to make love right then and there. I smiled at him instead of looking away. I fantasized about us leaving the livingroom and going upstairs to make love all evening and night. We did that often before we got married and before the babies were born. Since I had left Teddy, I had often fantasized about making love with him. He was a good lover.

Hours later, on the way home, Aunt Trina recollected the birthday parties that she and Uncle Clarence had given me. We laughed hysterically as she recalled the time one of the children knocked the cake off the table and I dived into it like it was Pudding Stone pond. The others followed right behind me.

"Lord, Jessi, you never did have good sense," she laughed.

After a long pause she said:

"Albert James reminds me of you so much. Looks like you spit him out. Yes, indeed, he was quite the little man today."

"Yes, he sure was. And wasn't he cute in those suspender pants? And Theodore. He was just too grown for me. What am I going to do when he turns five?"

"You looked happy today, Jessi."

"I think I was."

We actually are getting along as time passes, I thought. Albert James isn't such a bad child, and maybe I'm not such a bad mother.

There was silence for the first time. Then Aunt Trina said:

"Oh, Jessi. I saw the way Teddy was watching you today. He loves you so much. Why can't you straighten up?"

I didn't respond. I want to make my own decisions this time, I thought. I'm not going to give into their pressure.

"And he hasn't gone out and taken up with another woman. If he does, I can't say I would blame him," she said.

I wondered why she was being so indirect at this moment. Usually she referred to my relationship with Seye as "whoring around." She resented him and couldn't get over the fact that he was an African from Mali.

He's too pretty and too different," she said after meeting him for the first time. He had taken us to a French restaurant and she wasn't impressed a bit.

"What do you want with an African? You have nothing in common: not culture, not country, not generation, nothing. It's a godless shame for you two— does he know?"

"Yes, Aunt Trina. He knows that I'm separated from Teddy."

"Well, you're still married according to the law and in the eyes of God. He isn't as proper as he pretends to be if he carries on with another man's wife."

"He makes me feel free."

"Child, listen to me. You have to find your freedom deep within. Nobody else can make you free."

I knew she was right. But, I needed someone to confirm my desire to be more than a mother and a wife. I worked as a programmer but I didn't enjoy it. The salary was the only reason I kept the job.

Whenever I complained to Teddy about my unhappiness, he'd say:

"The money's good, Jessi. It's not such a bad job. Count your blessings."

He couldn't relate to my creative interests. When I told him I wanted a writing career, he said:

"There's no money in it. It's just pie-in-the-sky stuff, Jessi. Make it a hobby."

I wanted someone to accept every part of me and not consider me bizarre for wanting to write, regardless of the pay. Seye understood without any explanation. I was surprised, though, because I expected him to be the typical African chauvinist.

But he introduced me to Colette and Anais Nin. Often, after making love long into Saturday morning, we would discuss Nin's diaries and talk about her as if she was a personal friend.

Sometimes he'd lecture me on literature and philosophy as if I was one of his misguided students, but I loved it. Whatever he could teach me, I wanted to know. His genuine concern and his eagerness to love me far outweighed his

30

pompous manner.

We met in a downtown bookstore one evening six months ago. He introduced himself as a professor of literature. How arrogant, I thought. I then introduced myself as writer, although I wasn't yet convinced that I could actually be one.

"What do you write?" he asked as if he believed me.

"Stories."

"Yes, and about what?"

"About people and feelings and longings—"

"And do you long to be among the 'great' American writers?" he asked with serious eyes, but I detected slight mockery in his voice.

"I long to write well."

"Very good," he said smiling. "And so you will, my dear, you will."

Once after giving Seye a story to read, I awaited his response with the kind of excitement I remembered experiencing at eight years old as I anticipated the blooming of the first white roses I had planted with Uncle Clarence's help.

"I'm delighted to see that you're finally breaking free."

"But is it good?"

He walked over to his book shelf, taking down a book and skimming it.

"Here, Jessalyn, read this." He pointed to a passage in Nin's Novel of the Future. *It advised beginning writers not to rely on a critic to "decorate, bless or damn" them.*

I slammed the book down on the floor where I was sitting.

"I need you to tell me what you think. You know what's good and what isn't."

"Did you read what I just gave you?" he said.

"That's her opinion. I asked for yours."

"It's a good principle to stand on, Jessalyn. Suppose I told you that I don't like it? You would be crushed, wouldn't you? Then you may end up relying on my judgment and I may not ever like anything you write. But then again, someone else may come along and love what you write. Or vice versa."

He picked up the book and sat beside me, lifting my face toward his.

"You have great potential, so I don't want you to ever give up because of what anyone says, including me. I want you to be courageous, to be able to stand on your own. You understand me, Jessalyn?"

"No," I said just to be contrary. I felt angry and hurt.

We were almost home from the birthday party. After a period of silence I said:

"I'll go back, Aunt Trina, when I'm ready. Please don't push me."

"Is Seye the reason you're waiting so long?"

"No."

"I think it is, Jessi."

"He really has nothing to do with it."

"You think he gives you freedom, isn't that what you said? Don't be misled, child. You're not free. The devil has a hold of you," she said.

"Stop making me feel like I'm bad," I shouted. "And I'm sick of you running my life, Aunt Trina, I've let you do it this long and look where it's got me."

I drove into the driveway and parked the car. As I opened the door, she held my arm.

"Jessi, sugar, my heart grieves for you. I don't always understand you, but I believe that a person has to do what a person has to do, or else they'll go crazy. I believe that's what happened to you. You had to get out for a while; you needed to think things through. But you can't just think about yourself all the time. You have children. Teddy may not always be your husband but Albert James and Theodore Junior will always be your babies. Teddy has been acting like both a father and a mother to them. It's hard on him. Just like it would be hard on you if he left you to raise them alone. It's not fair. You have to make up your mind about either going back or leaving for good. And if you leave for good, you must consider those children."

"I know that. I'm trying to work it out," I said.

"I've known for a while that you love Seye, and Lord knows that you won't stop loving him if you go back to Teddy, and I'm not saying that you should. I know better. I learned long before you were born that people love more than one person at a time. Or that they may not love the one they're with but they stay any way for any number of reasons. You have to decide who you want to be with. You can't live with both of them in this world, Jessi."

She released my arm and we got out of the car.

"Hey, how about some hot chocolate?" she said as we walked into the house.

"If you spike it with some brandy."

"You've got a deal, sugar."

We stayed up late that night, drinking hot chocolate and thumbing through the family photo albums. Aunt Trina was in such a good mood, she read aloud some of the love letters that Uncle Clarence had written her while they dated and while he was away in the army during the first few years of their marriage.

It was the first time we had spent a nice evening together since I had moved in. I wondered what caused her to change her attitude so quickly but I didn't question her. I was just happy that it happened.

The following weekend, I drove to San Diego with Teddy and the boys. We went to the zoo and had a picnic lunch. Albert James was so well-behaved that I enjoyed spending the time with him. I was slowly getting over my apprehension about being around him. It turned out to be a pleasant, fun day.

The drive back to LaPuente was quiet, unlike the drive to San Diego. It was 9:30 p.m. and we were all exhausted. The boys were asleep in the back seat and I was half asleep, forcing myself to stay awake. I could tell by the way Teddy held his mouth that he was tired and in a plaintive mood. His lips were pressed together tightly and his jaw was taut. At times he looked as if he was going to cry.

We had been on the road for two hours before he said anything. Finally he spoke:

"Jessi, I love you, but I'm tired of this situation. You've got to decide which way you want it. Are you willing to be a full time mother and wife now or what? I need to know. You know, I use to think I couldn't make it without you. Now I know I can manage, as difficult as it is at times . . . I want you at home, *our* home, with us. If you're still not ready to come back and live your life with us—after all this time—then you'll never be, and we'll have to end this relationship. It's confusing to the boys and I'm sick of play the fool."

I was too tired to respond, and I really didn't know what to say. I had left so long ago that I, too, wondered if I'd ever return.

"As always you have nothing to say," he said.

"I'm trying to work through this," I said.

He didn't say anything else, so silence prevailed during the rest of the ride home.

We arrived at Aunt Trina's house at 10:45 p.m. I kissed the boys and thanked Teddy for the invitation. As I climbed out of the car, he said:

"You think about what I said tonight. You've had ample time to work through this thing. I want to know *soon* what you plan to do."

During the next month I stayed in Los Angeles to house sit for a friend vacationing in Europe. I didn't have contact with Teddy, Aunt Trina or Seye. I wanted to be completely alone. I need time and space to think without being influenced by any of them.

When I returned to LaPuente, I called Seye.

"How are you, Jessalyn?"

"Tired."

"Must have been an exciting vacation."

"No, actually I did nothing but think a lot."

"What kind of vacation is that?" he said, laughing.

"A much needed one. Actually I was just out of town. I still had to work, you know."

"You sound like you need your spirits lifted. How about dinner? I just bought a nice duckling—"

"No, Seye. I'm not hungry. I'll see you soon."

When I let myself in, Seye's place was dimly lit with candles. The air smelled of Gonesh incense, No. 6, my favorite. David Sanborn's alto sax lured me into the study where Seye sat low on a queen-sized futon.

"Come here," he said, his words feeling like his soft fingers that often caressed my lips. When I reached him, he pulled me forward and kissed each eyelid. The slight pressure of his mouth caused my eyes to tingle.

When the tears came, he licked my cheeks.

"Mmm . . . tastes like the North Sea," he said, smacking his lips. We both laughed; he was always good for a laugh in such inappropriate times.

He pulled me down and I folded into his slender arms. I sank down on the futon beside him, though he had meant for me to sit on his lap. Our long, nibbling kisses indicated that we wanted to make love. I broke away.

My tears felt cool against my cheeks. I had left traces on his face. When I lifted a hand to wipe away the dampness, he stopped me. He reached for my hand and pressed it against his mouth. I curled my fingers around his thumb and held on tightly.

"No, don't," he said. "I want my pores to drink it. I want whatever I can get from you right now."

I lay my head in his lap and cried until I heaved and felt nauseated. He played with my hair, wrapping strands around his fingers. At times he would try to life my head, but I wouldn't let him see my face. It felt ugly, distorted. It was drenched, and my eyes felt swollen.

When I finally raised my head, I looked away, standing up abruptly. I went to the bathroom to blow my nose. On the vanity was a delicate crystal perfume bottle. It's top was shaped like a dove. The bottle was was filled with *Inoui*, my favorite fragrance. A white rose was tied to its neck with a white, satin ribbon. A tiny card was propped against it:

"Pour toi, mon amour. Je t'aime et je t'aimerai toujours."

"je t'aime pour tonjours," I wrote on the mirror in lipstick.

I walked around the apartment, collecting odds and ends of my world, hoping to make it whole. Seye remained in the study the entire time. When I returned, he had on ear phones and was stretched across the futon, resting on his stomach. I couldn't see his face. I kneeled down and kissed the back of his neck. Sitting there for a few moments, I stared into his back. I then stood up and left the room.

I removed his apartment key from my key ring and placed it on the vanity in the bathroom. After turning off all the lights I had turned on earlier, I stepped out into the bright corridor and started down the stairs.

MAGIC

Essie Caldwell Kammin

You made
       it possible for a stranger
       to enter my life—
       to shatter dreams,
       displace pleasant memories
       to break the almost perfect facade,
       only a lie,
       that had been weaved
       into magic.

The sound
       of your voice
       now but a dim
       memory.

Faded photographs
       in the dungeon
       of my mind—
       bring troubling thoughts
       of our times.

Yesterday
       when I wore
       a young girl's ribbons,
       bright, rainbow colors
       of you, filled my life.

Today
       wearing the perfume
       of a woman,
       the dazzling colors
       are gone—
       replaced by bleak
       scenes of winter
       filled with dirty snow.

As you
    lie buried beneath coconuts
    palms and hisbiscus,
    your secret sins
    have reached out
    to taunt me.

Laying on of Hands   Ta-coumba T. Aiken '84

TRAINS

LaNette

She pulled her chair closer to the wooden table and looked past the bareness of the room through the wired window. The snow was falling heavier now. She could hear the scratching sound of ice scrapped from a car window, a distant motor failing to ignite. Winter. So cruel. So merciless. She cleared her throat. And again. And nervously lit a cigarette from the pack Woyansky had laid on the table. Woyansky. Not an unkind looking man. He looked tired. A tired looking man in a neatly tailored suit. He sat against the wall waiting for her to begin. Woyansky. She wondered what his life was like. What his dreams were. Woyansky. She wondered if he hated her. Silence.

"Can I have a cup of coffee?"

He looked startled. He moved with effort towards the door and motioned at the police officer behind it. Silence. The door opened and closed again. A styrofoam cup of black coffee. His seat at the table across from her now. He stared at her with expressionless eyes—waiting.

"Where was she?" She thought absently.

She wrapped her hands around the cup and enjoyed the warmth of the pungent liquid going down her throat. She felt so cold. Cold and alone.

"I used to think I always hated him," she began aloud to herself. "Even when he was a baby. Just a little baby." Her voice trailed off. She glanced around the room. Woyansky's accusing glare. Empty. A barren room in the midst of nothingness. Had she always been there?

"Have you ever heard of anyone hating a baby?" Pause. "I did. I don't know why. I had thought it wouldn't be so bad at first—when he was a baby. My baby." She smiled to herself. "You know, he really was a good baby. He never cried. When he was little, he would play by himself."

She stared out of the window at the winter sky. It was just November. Snow in November. A long, long time before spring.

Next month was her birthday. And Christmas. She had planned for the two of them to spend Christmas with her mother. She hadn't seen her mother in three years. Three years can be half a lifetime. Christmas three years ago. Her mind drifted. It had taken nine and one half hours on a cramped greyhound bus. He had slept most of the way. It had seemed so strange going back there. To Chicago. Home. It was so far away. A shrunken grey lady in a crowd. "This is your grandma. Can you say 'grandma?'" She held him in her arms. But of course he wouldn't say "grandma." Not even "hello."

Woyansky looked at his watch. A graduation gift. It was almost 4:00. Rush hour. Rushing, rushing in the outside world. He had promised the psychiatrist at the neighborhood mental health center that he would be on time. Time for an appointment over an old storefront. Dressed in a tailored suit.

Woyansky. Public defender. A tired, useless joke. Woyanksy. Champion of none. His mind rambled. Maybe he should start to jog again? Or go to the gym more often? Or breathe more often? Something. Anything. Everything seemed so meaningless.

"When he was almost one," she said flatly, "the doctor said there was something wrong with his feet. Something about being turned in the wrong way. He had to wear heavy casts nearly up to his hips for months. And I had to carry him. He was so heavy. But I took care of him. I used to drop him off at the babysitter's on my way to work and pick him up on my way home in the evening. I never had a ride." She spoke in a monotone. "That's why he was so late walking. Because of the casts. He used to drag himself around the apartment. Like a seal. Drag himself like a damn animal. I would come home from work and there'd he go, dragging himself around on the dirty floor. On the damn dirty floor with the bugs."

He looked into her face. It was angry, hardened. From her life? From the lack of it? Query. She was only 23. Where had he been when he was 23? It seemed like centuries ago. Where would he be when he was 30. Or 40. Where would she be. His temples pounded. Still outside the window, it snowed.

He had called her mother last night. At his own insistence. Because she should know. Because maybe she could help. He had held the phone dumbly while an old woman cried her daughter's tears. He gave no words of reassurance. He knew none. He had lit a cigarette while a woman he had never met cried into the phone long distance. She had told Woyansky that she would come for the arraignment. He didn't have to ask.

And again silence. Still the snow. Falling madly, blindly, striking viciously, from a remorseless sky. An old woman crying five hundred miles away. A young woman smoking filterless cigarettes. A son's haunted eyes. Irony.

"I haven't seen his father since I was pregnant. He never asked about his father. Strange. When I went to the hospital to have him, the nurse asked me his name. The name of my baby's father. I told her it didn't matter. The father was a bastard and the baby would be a bastard too. The nurse just stared at me. She looked young. She just stared." Her voice cracked. A vacant face. Distant. "My son. He was all I ever had. And he never knew." She strained for composure. "I gave him those toy trains they found in his pocket. One day we went shopping. I bought them for him. It was a surprise. I paid for them without him knowing. After dinner, I gave them to him. He was so surprised. Tiny, toy trains." Her voice was shaking. She was shivering. "He loved trains. He would watch them pass from his bedroom window. My son."

Her soliloquy. To her son. "I went to the neighborhood mental health center last summer. I was so depressed. I don't know why. I went on my own. Nobody made me go. The first thing the doctor asked me was if I ever hit my baby. I told him 'no'. I could tell he didn't believe me. He put me into a group with women who had problems dealing with their children. Some of them would beat their kids. They would say so. One woman had her baby taken away. We would meet every Thursday night. I never had much to say."

Woyansky looked at his client. She looked a great deal like the picture he had seen of the boy. A small boy with unblinking, staring eyes. The police had found his body just three hours after she had reported him late for school. They found him bludgeoned to death. Wrapped in a dirty burlap sack. A lonely little boy. They found him less than a quarter of a mile from his home on the side of the railroad tracks. Amid the rubble. Oblivious to the roar of the engines in his ears.

CHRISTMAS TALE

Conrad Balfour

He filled the bowl with hot water and soap, then dipped the dishes and cups into it. Instead of rinsing them in a water-catch he held them under the faucet. He knew that it was wasteful. The dishwasher was loaded and when the sink was cleared he attached the hose and turned on the controls. He let the dishes that he had handwashed dry upon the counter. Now he carried the litterbag out back and dropped it into a can. He heard glass tinkle as the sack fell. He had broken two wine glasses in the sink. A few days before that a wine glass shattered as he polished it. So thin.

There were guests three consecutive evenings and he had tidied the house each day. Dinner, card party, party. Ruth washed clothes, cooked. The understanding was that he monitored dishes. The arrangement worked.

He was disturbed at himself. The first night he stayed up late cleaning. He put bowls in the cupboard, crackers in the bin, glasses and dishes in the pantry. Heavy mugs sat on an oak counter awaiting their turn. As he picked them up with his fingers serving as hooks, he noticed a water stain. One bottom hadn't dried and a towel was of no help.

Two days later he did the same. Ruth left a note: There are more rings. Have a nice day. I love you.

He looked on the dressers. Upstairs had nine of them. He searched his overcoat pockets, jean jacket, workshirt. Not on the bathroom sink, the counter, nor at bedside. He was certain that he had worn the Seiko that morning. When he jogged he timed the 2.8 miles around the lake. Twenty eight minutes. He sighed concession and felt his wrist. There it was.

The tree was exotic. Tiny beads of red and pink, green and yellow. Before Ruth returned he placed three presents beneath it. He couldn't wrap well but enjoyed plastering tape over paper. Other packages were done by Macy's Gift Wrap. The middle-aged woman remembered him from the year before. She beamed at the soft coat that he had purchased.

When he slid the brown package close to the base the tree tilted forward. He caught a center limb and worked it upright. They had cut the pine on Sunday. Drove fifty miles in mild weather. Gas was expensive and the tree was only six dollars.

That evening Ruth watered the treestand and the pine tilted again. He held it steady as she tightened the stays. They snapped at each other as they hovered over the gifts.

At night the tree filled the house with reflections. The bookcase threw a muted collage into the den. The sunroom bent the colors around the north corner. Before company arrived he jogged the lake and cried at the beauty that spilled onto the east shore. The sky fanned pink, clung like a half-shell onto the receded sun and dabbed the water not yet frozen. Quiet country. His breath jumped at each pace. He recalled Ruth's description of her jog over this same path during the first snowfall. The light flakes fell into her eyes and her legs danced through the showers. Then she had witnessed a sunset from the car, over the river, a fall of amber above South Dakota. It stayed with her. Both of them were stocking up on majestic sights.

When Tara looked up he was pushing the door open. "Daddy." She was four. He panted into the living room. The tree was there. She was coloring a paper and stopped to smile. He was stunned by her eyes. He crouched next to her and said, "let me see." The green in her face radiated and he shook his head. "Where's the brown? It's gone." She lowered her eyes to the colors and whispered, "daddy."

He caught his breath and began to sing. "Chestnuts roasting in an open fire."

"Stop, Daddy."

"Why? Did I get the wrong words again?"

"Stop."

"Do you love me?"

"Yes but—I get a heachache when you sing."

The company enjoyed the evening. One guest sat alone for a time. He wore strong black shoes and long underwear hugged above them. His face was sturdy and good and his fingers were thick like the kindling wood in the shed. He said his worked for the Park Department. In all his years he had never had a week like this one. "Kids vandalized the warmin' house. Tore out boards. Mus' a been a crowbar. Tire iron maybe. Windows were burst proof and they knew it. Broke into the room and burnt them. That's one thing them windows aint. They can catch fire. Sure can."

Tim had a full plate. Rice, sticks of meat, pink salad. He had been called by a California pollster for the Gallup people. They interviewed him for 45 minutes about Lebanon. "I used to wonder who those people were that they called. Never matched my views. Now here I am—interviewed. I took ten pages of notes so that I could review what they asked."

Alex had a 16 year old Egyptian lad at his place. He was proud of the experience. His foot was heavy and it brushed up and down to a branch of the tree as he beamed with each story. "Hard adjustment. Women are regarded in a different manner. Calls me dad. His own father means so much to him. Before Sadat was killed he'd see him on television and sit bolt upright. They loved Sadat."

Tara played upstairs with Shawn. Shawn's parents attempted to put him to sleep, but music from the Nutcracker Suite interfered. More than that Tara would not cooperate. Shawn's dad was exhausted from the tribulation and Ruth was upset with our daughter.

He looked at the windows behind the sofa. His company bobbed their heads over white cups of coffee. The windows glowed. He had washed them from the outside that morning. Washed windows in the winter. It seemed silly to him, but on the ladder he saw a white squirrel. It was a fine omen.

When the last friend kissed them goodnight, Ruth got into her nightgown and climbed under the comforter. He picked up napkins and shook crumbs, scraped and poured dregs, nibbled at peanut brittle and loaded the washer. He returned wine to the basement, restored the antique chairs to their places, failed at fitting a wing to the dining room table. He closed the damper in the fireplace but it was premature. The room filled with the smell of ashes. Outdoors on the walkway he pondered over 25 sacks that had votive candles anchored in sprinkles of sand. He decided to allow them the night. They were elegant and added a fairy tale dimension to the street. Inside he paused a few moments at the tree, the gifts under it. Then he touched the light switch and climbed the stairs to Ruth and Tara.

He spread sliced meats upon blue and white plates, slabs of cheese, Coors beer, pumpernickel, ginger cookies and spiced mustard. The card game halted as the six men prepared their plates. They sat by the tree and talked of peers, retired professors and the state of affairs. He loved them, but all he could offer (and it came as an announcement)—"what a fine group we are."

When the game resumed he concentrated on a diamond flush. The men were exchanging jokes and he warmed at the laughter. He concentrated so hard on his hand that he heard only snatches;—

"Cast the first stone ..."

"Life lies in the breast of pheasants ..."

"... and the pope said, 'the immorality of divorce' ..."

When they departed, Arthur lingered at the door. "Want you over. We'll ski. Do a few things." They were close. Very close.

When he crawled into the comforter he felt a numb pain in his testes. Two years ago his doctor had examined him there and had told him that one day he'd have trouble. He thought of that now. Curiously enough he also thought of the rust stain in the large English bathtub, the church bells that rang out earlier. What church was it? He thought of Tara's grandmother and her struggle to comb a ponytail. He thought of lox and cream cheese, failing vision, Ruth calling from the bedroom as he descended the stairs; "I love you." He noticed that she emphasized each word as if to be certain that he understood.

Santa hung from the limb of the pine tree. A donkey. A clown. A giraffe. A crimson heart. He switched it off.

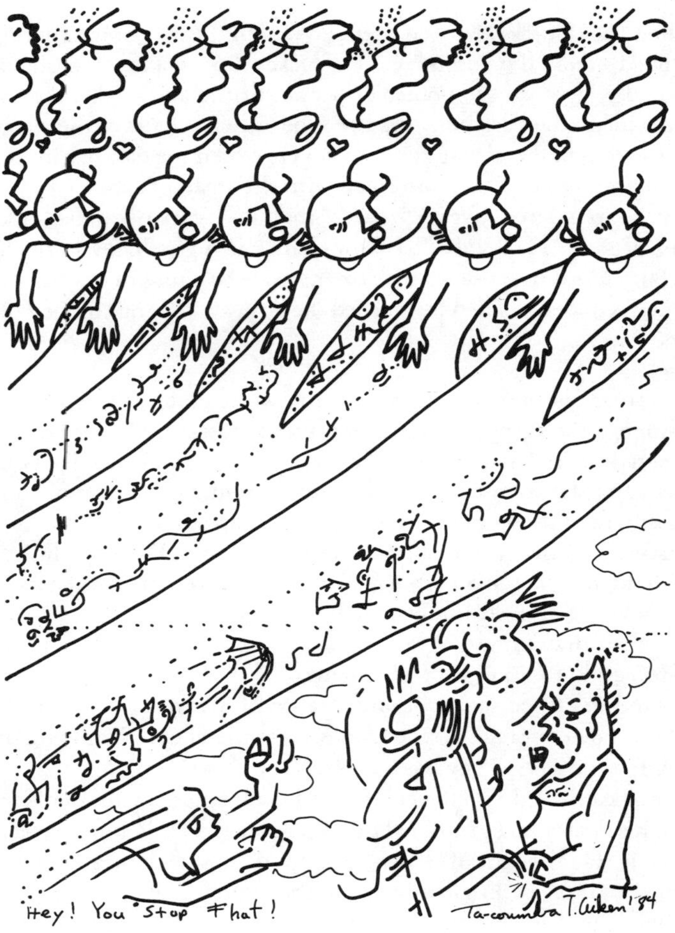
Hey! You Stop that!
Ta-coumba T. Aiken '84

FROM MY JOURNAL
June 14, 1981
DIALOGUE BETWEEN THE WRITER AND A CHARACTER

Carolyn Holbrook-Montgomery

WRITER: I'm afraid of you, Pepper.

CHARACTER: I know you are. Everytime you try to write about me you end up sitting in your writing chair agonizing over me until you finally change your mind and write about the weather or just give up and go eat some fat makers.

WRITER: I don't understand where the fear comes from.

CHARACTER: Oh yes you do. It's perfectly obvious to me.

WRITER: Oh yeah? Well then explain it to me.

CHARACTER: I'll do nothing of the kind. Figure it out for yourself. Remember, you're the one who wants to dredge me up out of the baser corners of your mind. I didn't ask you to create me.

WRITER: When I started this crappy story all I wanted was to tell the truth about George. I wasn't all that interested in you.

CHARACTER: (Laughs sarcastically) Idiot! Know what I think?

WRITER: I'm afraid to ask.

CHARACTER: I think this story is really about you.

WRITER: About me? Oh come on, Pepper. I wouldn't think of being a hooker.

CHARACTER: Wouldn't you?

WRITER: No. Of course not. You know me better than that.

CHARACTER: Do I?

WRITER: Of course you do. What would Mom and Dad think of me? What would Aunt Madge think of me?

CHARACTER: They don't seem to think a whole lot of you anyway.

WRITER: You got that right.

CHARACTER: Listen, sugar. When you come right down to it, you've been a prostitute all your life.

WRITER: That's a lie. If it were true I wouldn't be so damned poor. I wouldn't have submitted to that insidious marriage that left me in this sorry condition.

CHARACTER: Really?

WRITER: Really!!

CHARACTER: Why'd you marry him?

WRITER: You know why I married him.

CHARACTER: Of course I do. But that wasn't my question.

WRITER: Well .. when you're young, gifted and black and you're trying to raise a kid by yourself and you have dreams of becoming a famous Broadway actress ...

CHARACTER: Hold it! Don't go no further! Look. I realize that a lot of what you were about to say is true. But for you, my dear, it's the ultimate cop out.

WRITER: What do you mean?

CHARACTER: After the film you knew success was a definite possibility and the whole idea of success freaked you out. You also knew that marriage to B. would give you 100% assurance that success would never happen. You refused to let go of the failure syndrome you had come to love and depend on. Hooker!! Prostitute!! Whore!!

WRITER: Hey. Slow down, Pepper. Aren't you exaggerating just a tad?

CHARACTER: Think about it. Why didn't you marry W. or A.? They both loved you and were very supportive of the things you wanted to do. Why didn't you opt for independence and find your own way?

WRITER: Well, I ... I ...

CHARACTER: Hey. I thought this conversation was supposed to be about me.

*   *   *   *   *

UNTITLED

Carolyn Holbrook-Montgomery

Winter again
Why
Death
Burial grounds in winter
Daddy King
died this week
George Bush spoke at his funeral
Why
Cold blood
C.I.A.
Baboon heart killed Baby Fae
Turn up the heat
It's cold in here

AT THE COFFEE SHOP

Carolyn Holbrook-Montgomery

A few moments alone with myself
to sip coffee and listen to jazz
to reflect on love and inner peace
and rejoice in the oneness of me
I look up, the place is suddenly crowded
my peaceful moment gone

Wish he'd come in
his blue eyes, tranquil
like a clear lake in springtime
suggest re-awakening of
passions thought dead

Brother said, "Black is beautiful,"
"My queen, I greet you,"
The blue-eyed man is the devil"
Brother walks in with two blondes,
glances my way, turns his head, says
"Ain't wastin' my energy on no black bitch!"

Tired of being alone
Energy crisis
Tired of wasting my energy
Ain't wastin' no more energy

WHISTLING WOMAN

Soyini Guyton

*A whistling woman and a crowing
hen don't never come to a good end.*

"Your Aunt Lovey," my grandfather said, "is a fast, ruthless vagabond, barren as a rock, black as soot, and she never tells the truth unless it's by accident. Occasionally she'll intentionally tell the truth but that's just in order to confuse or mislead. That woman'll lie even when the truth would serve her better.

"Of all my children she was the hardest to raise. The only one I had to whip. Nothing seemed to satisfy her. No answer was ever complete enough for her. When she was little I whipped her everytime she'd ask me who made God until she stopped asking. I whipped her for wearing nail color, for wearing her hair loose and shaking it, for switching her hips like some old mare, for wearing lipstick, for snapping her fingers and dancing, for owning a deck of cards, for cutting her eyes at grownups and for having too much lip. I whipped her for whistling, too. I can't stand to hear a woman whistle. It unnerves me. She stopped all that other foolishness but wouldn't stop whistling. After awhile she was too grown to be whipping on so she did what no woman in my house, or my father's house had ever done: she whistled. Whenever she felt like it, too.

"When she left here she said she'd never live under another roof where she'd have to dance to a tune other than her own. She'd done plenty of dancing under this roof because I *had* to whip her just to keep her in line. Lovey was always arguing and questioning and challenging anything and anybody.

"Looking back I see how I encouraged her, but she was a child then and I didn't see any harm in it. But when she started asking all those questions I couldn't answer, things I never even thought about, I started whipping her to put some shame and fear in her heart.

"When she was six years old, she became fascinated with the idea of a pot of gold at the end of the rainbow. She'd go looking for it. We, me and your grandmother, indulged her because, then, we liked her curiosity and intelligence. We were proud of her. The children of our friends and relatives, our other children too, seemed dull and unimaginative compared to her. They weren't. It just seemed that way because Lovey had so much life in her. Some people come into this world with hardly enough vitality to sustain them. Others, like Lovey, got hers and that of somebody else.

"Well, this curiosity and vitality set her to thinking that she would be the one to discover the pot of gold.

"All that summer when she was six, whenever there was a rainbow, she'd be off looking for the pot of gold. We'd pack her a lunch and watch her walk away.

She was so pretty, especially her legs. Strong legs. She never forgot to stop before she rounded the bend and wave good bye to us. That child was loved.

"She went searching for that pot of gold until she was eight years old; we went on packing her a lunch and encouraging her.

"When she was ten, she began looking around closer to home with questions. That's when the trouble began. She started acting like she didn't have the sense she was born with. Like she'd been raised by no accounts. She was smart as a ship. Could've been a school teacher, like her sister, she was so smart. But I knew, even then, that she'd never amount to anything.

"True to her word, she's never lived long under anyone's roof. It wasn't long before she bought herself a house. She's owned her house for a long time now. Bought herself a car, too. She ain't never had to do without, not even during the real hard times. Of course she had something that sold when cotton and corn didn't.

"Bought a camera and went off to the World Fair, *alone*. Always getting pictures made of *herself*. That woman is vain. Proud and vain. Pride and vanity comes before a fall. And not even bothering to think about getting married.

"Now she's sick. Got that disease that eats you all up inside and drives you crazy with pain."

I willed myself to become a still, mute stone, for had I moved, I would've crumbled. Aunt Lovey had been sick but no one told me she had cancer. I imagined masses of maggots in a carcass. I wanted to protest in loud discordant unruly sounds and words. I felt like doing something with substance, with weight. Something that would carry the pain I felt. I wanted to hit my grandfather in the stomach, like kids do to each other, and knock the wind out of him.

We were sitting under a shade tree, I on the bench built into the trunk of the tree and he in his rocking chair. He'd been talking with his eyes closed, hands folded across his stomach and rocking slowly. Every once in a while he'd jut out his chin and scratch his beard or sniff at the air as if he were trying to pick a scent off the wind. His eyes were squeezed shut; his nostrils flared dangerously.

"You understand, don't you," grandfather asked, "that a woman can't carry herself like a man? Not in this world nor the next. All a man got to lose is his reputation. A woman loses her reputation and her character." His eyes fluttered, then opened. His gaze, though sympathetic and warm, left no room for contradiction.

A leaf from the shade tree came gliding through the air, sauntering almost, slid over my forehead, cheeks and lips leaving streamers of excitement, fear and anger in its wake. Thoughts of Aunt Lovey and her illness, grandfather's manner of presenting it to me, and the thrill the sauntering leaf left on me crowded my mind. I was pushed beyond my capacity to separate and channel. I began to cry with such force that the first tears jumped straight from my eyes onto my lap.

Grandfather's razor edge didn't waver. It hung between us just like the axe in the shed hung between the shovel and the hoe. He wrinkled his forehead and said, "You'd better save those tears, because one of these days you're going to have something to cry about. Your Aunt Lovey is a hard-headed woman. Acting mannish. Always whistling. A whistling woman and a crowing hen don't never come to a good end."

What is this thing about whistling women that unnerves my grandfather? Is whistling sacred or profane? If sacred, why was it set aside as a male only activity? If profane, who's showing contempt for whom? The woman who whistles despite the warning, or the environment that issues the warning?

Grandfather whistled all the time. Whenever and wherever he felt the urge: in the bathroom, as he cooked, while dressing, driving, shopping and in church. He couldn't sing but he whistled strong, vibrant, many textured melodies.

If he wanted to mock a phony or absurd situation, he'd whistle a melody of subtle and searing humor, or something jaunty when he felt really terrific, or a silly, simple, repetitive tune those times he'd decide that we wouldn't work for the whole day. We'd pretend we were ne'er do wells just living off the fat of the land. When we took pears from Mrs. Lee's pear tree, we'd stop to visit her, then be on our way. As we walked away, there'd be a sneaky, light rhythm to his step. He'd whistle "Pop Goes the Weasel" real slow while winking at me. I think he loved pretending to be the trickster. After grandmother died, his melodies, for a while, were weak and translucent from aching and longing. Whistling has been a companion to him, a good steady one at that. A companion not proper, he thought, for a woman.

Don't Let Go Mommy!!!   Ta-coumba T. Aiken '85

FIVE BLACKS ENTERING A ROOM

Donald Govan

Blown in black like a prairie
storm through the torn flap
of a plains teepee.
The room's light flashes
brilliant Black smiles warm
as the glow of mother's face
when father's presence lit
the room bright as one
thousand diamonds.
Silent waves of vibrancy
pop and spin throughout the
room with the invisible energy
that makes colts wild and
sends unbroken Black boys
to penitentiaries.
One begins to think of fire
and power and greatness.
One begins to think that
perhaps it wasn't god Prometheus
robbed ...
One begins to know satisfaction:
that Prometheus stole so
little.

VISION

Donald Govan

I live
in the eye
of coyotes.
We stare over
barren beauty-
short cactus-
tough grass.
We weep
and turn to
deeper cover.

CHRYSALIS

Donald Govan

I was a 7 year old man
when Aunt Mae died.
Cool as morning earth
I said: "Gee, when is
the funeral?"
    If she could
    see me now ...
    This man ...
I carried her coffin
box with the men; who
appeared more proud on
this occasion.
I rode straight up in
the negligible dignity
of a big cadillac.
    I'm a warrior performing
    the death ritual.

At the grave, I stood
tall as Indians I had
seen idling outside
South Dakota taverns.
My pride soared like the
little sparrow
making curious swoops
over the gathering.
Meaningless words were
spoken
and people began to leave.
I stayed; watching workmen
pick up shovels.
The pebbles plinked against
the steel;
making empty sounds that
cracked my manhood wide
open;
like the split head of
a foolish john found dead
in the alley on Sunday
morning.
My last piece of childhood
fell out in an uncontrolable
sob.
Melted into terrible tears.
I saw all I thought I
knew
buried under the dirt of Aunt
Mae's gravehole.
Now it's all over ...
I'm a child for life.

COURAGE

Donald Govan

I saw Crazy Horse's
great vision
counting coup
down Franklin ave.

drunk;

smiling at people
and
joking with children.

Down that ugly street
he staggered.

A death chant under his
breath
prepared for resurrection

beside great spirits
and a brave warrior's
rage.

RUFUS
For Tom Govan, Dee Dee, Don, etc.

Donald Govan

Now there is no form
to slip into,
but there never was.
Goddamn! I'll go to the
shadows
and make nothing of
images.
They are the statement
of meaning.

That fucking devil is
a dam.
Let me flood him; drown
him.

Hearing the soul over
burdened with voice.
Heavy blue voice:
bleeding from eternal
castration:
stirring the women;
Black women, White women.
Goddamn you!
Their thighs speak of my
function;
my assertion,
and my tears as they
wiggle out the door
smiling.

My violence
after the liquor ritual
the reefer smoke
curling ...

I'll do tricks for the
children
or
go down the street to show
the other women,
get her money
and cry
watching her wiggle out
the door smiling.

The unintentional contempt
in mother's black pool eyes:
chronic want.

Wistfully
seeing father's beautiful
grin in mine.
"A pretty man, but no good.
Don't be like your Daddy."
Daddy's resentment glows in me.

Down to the other women
and
sleep ... dreaming ...
Black with a hammer smashing
Cadillacs
screaming motherfuckers
motherfuckers
you dirty motherfuckers.
Blasting wine bottles,
smashing the mirrors reflecting
the ludicrous reefer grin.
Walking straight, no bullshit.
Get back motherfuckers.
Children behind, mamas
frightened.
Safe, I'm making it safe.

Awake
the wine reefer pushing away
the child's voice ...
Daddy ...
saying; study child. Be
something.
Staring at the floor,
closing my eyes to dream of
women
obliterating the child's face ...
my face, daddy's face ...
trying to believe it wasn't
a lie.
Study child, just study.

Love them Mama, I must
get drunk,
hide — to think
about another drink,
another drag, another
woman.

Standing on the bridge:
water looks evil,
looks free ...
I'm goddamn tired
of averted eyes, children's
eyes, women's eyes,
my eyes.
The river slime now washes
the eyes
my eyes
looking with no eyes no
flesh
for that spirit whimpering
in Hell but gaining strength
in death land, where possibility
exists.

THE BUTTERFLY TREE

Alexs D. Pate

Certain tears stream down her face. Some evaporate in the stinging August sun. The rest flow free form down her soft cheeks. Her cheeks, instantly tense, like hardening brown clay, capture her spirit. The tears collect at the curve of her chin like ants on a drop of honey left on a picnic table.

She has never passed through those thin veils of time which can transform a free soul into a mushy goo which no longer cares to search for dreams.

Her voice is only soft in the morning. At night, when she is near sleep, the sounds she makes are throaty, heavy, as if she were struggling against her body to make words.

This morning the sun shines upon her and turns to shards of bursting color as it careens off the curled dry leaves lining the path she walks. Unknown to her this light envelopes her and renders this young woman a vision to the field mice that scamper to the cover of a hollow log five feet away.

And a vision she remains as her heels come down upon the dead leaves. There are so many lying there, and many more falling around her that the small space taken up by her shoes as they touch the earth do not bespeak the mutilation. She remains unaware. And those leaves falling around her, they come down slowly, lazily, almost blissfully as if the fall itself was their autumnal orgasm; hoped for and awaited with eagerness. Yet, within this world of trees and changing lives, the fall of those leaves was as violent as any mass murder and the growing accumulation of lifeless leaves was as chilling as a heap of dead bodies taken from Soweto.

She knew nothing of this.

For twenty two summers this path had been hers. Ten of them she had travelled alone. The first twelve she faced with a man she watched die.

Luther Brown walked with a smooth saunter. A stroll. He wore his red pants cuffed and three inches above the tops of his shoes. Never to be seen in public without suspenders and a white shirt, Luther Brown sported an impeccably kept black derby.

To be sure, Luther Brown was perhaps the only man in the state who felt comfortable with a black derby on his head on a hot August day. He had a reputation for style. Nobody's matched his.

In the twelve years since Luther died, Lillian kept to her promise. She walked the path. It was a painful ordeal. It left her weak and afraid. Every year it would be three, maybe four months after the fearful journey before she could sleep a full night's sleep. They weren't nightmares as much as feelings of dread. This dread haunted her. Sometimes it was presented in forms she was very familiar with. Sometimes dread visited her as her father. A dead man.

There were times though, that Lillian woke in flash of sweat running from

62

her body, trembling like a tulip in the wind, knowing dread as a different form. As a monster. Perhaps a flicker of light.

Early October in Minnesota is a time when people begin to think of cold weather. The behavior of people at this time mirrored that of the smaller life moving around her. There was much movement to prepare for the harsh weather ahead. The mind changes to adapt. As the days grow shorter, more clothes are rescued from the odor of mothballs. One brings winter along like a wagon laden with logs for splitting.

She wore a sweater as if it were a cape, with the arms tied around her neck and the body of the garment softly flapping against her back. A blue cotton sweater with white buttons. Her favorite.

Luther Brown told her always to wear something blue. It was his second favorite color. He said it brought out the soft brown tones on her face. He said black folks looked good in blue.

Luther took his colors seriously. Lillian nearly forgot that. And so on each October first, as she trudged through the ever increasing cushion of dead leaves, she was sure to have something on which was blue, her given color. Luther had given it to her.

A good man, Luther was not completely selfless. He kept his favorite color for himself. Luther wore red. Except for his hat and his shirt, Luther would dress in his given color, particularly his pants. Luther had more shades of red pants than Gloria Vanderbilt.

Lillian was Luther's daughter although he had left her and her mother six months after she was born. As far back as she could remember, Luther had been gone. Twice a year he would find them. If they moved, he found them. On Christmas eve for twelve years running, he found them.

Her mother charged apartments rather frequently. Lillian had never understood it. Her mother never explained. They would live in a place for six or seven months, everything would seem fine and suddenly on returning from school one day, she would trip over boxes and shopping bags filled with their possessions, all neatly awaiting transport to some new shelter. So being found was of some significance.

On Christmas eve, Luther would call them (he somehow always managed to get the telephone number as well) and ask if he could come and see Lillian. When she would open the door, he'd be standing there, grinning, arms full of wrapped packages and smelling like a rose garden.

No matter how she felt, on Christmas Eve, Luther would bring her happiness. It didn't matter how long he stayed, or what they did; he *made* Christmas for her.

But on October first, she knew, without any doubt whatsoever, that Luther would call and ask to take her for a ride. She'd get dressed, find a nice blue skirt or a blue jacket and head off with him in a rusted 68 chevrolet.

They would ride through the city of Minneapolis, going from north to south and out into the suburbs. They would ride for about a half hour on the highway before Luther would turn into a rest stop area to drink a beer and to let Lillian have a snack. She always ate the same thing, coca cola and Lance's crackers with peanut butter in the middle.

Soon they'd be on the road again. Passing, as they drove, field after field of shriveled corn stalks, empty, retired and destined for hog slop. The harvest corn could be spotted occasionally laying in baskets at roadside markets.

Her tears know their terrain. She keeps careful count. Lillian is not anxious to bear too much pain. She will limit it this time. Luther had opened this world to her and she felt compelled to keep her promise to him.

They would slow near Northfield. His eyes would begin to narrow, as he now became someone she had at first feared, then, later understood, sympathized with.

They would leave the car and begin their hike through a small wooded area. It remained unchanged year after year.

"It is gone."

"I don't believe you," Lillian said in a fairly shrill voice which captured the emotion tinged by the remnants of her tears. She was gaining strength. She knew what was ahead.

As they walked, Luther would usually find a small branch to aid his balance as they moved through the woods. And he would begin to talk about his life. His story came out in bursts of laughter and fresh sounding voice. It seemed he covered so much distance in such short time.

In no time Lillian would know all the details of the past year. Where he had been, what he had done, and who he had done it to. One year he was wanted by the police. The next by a girlfriend he had taken money from. He told her everything. He told her quickly.

As he talked he would continuously jerk his head upward as if pointing to the path before them. Sometimes he would stop and caution her to keep still and they would just stand there and listen. Then, with equal spontaneity, he would begin walking and talking again.

Luther grew up in Minneapolis. He grew up shoveling snow for quarters. He grew up in a world that was whiter than it had a right to be. Greater than its sum, Minnesota and its culture quickly enclosed Luther, as it did other blacks, in a web of self doubt and confusion.

This was a land where opportunity was abundantly manifest yet devastatingly illusive to those of a darker life. In this wake Luther became himself. He chose red because he felt warm with it on. Even in the winter. Those around him watched askance.

As he got older he became someone who people learned to feel sorry for. There were hushed whisperings about him. His pants. His derby. His disappearing. His visits to Lillian. Their trips. His visions.

He wouldn't keep them to himself. For some reason, he wanted everyone to know. During the summer, when he was in the city, Luther would stroll out on to Plymouth Avenue, dressed in his fashion, and attempt to explain himself to anyone who would listen.

"Some people know more my friend. Some people are given more to work with. Some of us can walk past the shadows and the darkness that separates people like you from the truth. I have seen the other side. I have walked over there. Know the truth my brothers. Know the truth."

The whispers stopped. People now knew. When someone changes from quiet transcendental visions to buttonholing people on the street to talk about "the other side" a community becomes itself, a cultural fortress. Instead of whispers there was now laughter.

Luther would talk about this with Lillian.

"They did the same thing to Christ."

"What?" Lillian at eleven.

"That's why they laugh at me. They can't accept the truth. You'll understand. One day it will be yours." Luther took his hat off and wiped his brow with a large red handkerchief he kept rolled into a rather forebodingly tight ball. Whenever he pulled it from his pocket, he would wave it in the air like a flag and either wipe his forehead or blow his nose. Then he'd roll it up tightly again and stuff it into his pocket.

"Mine? What?"

"The butterfuly tree."

"That can't be mine," Lillian said, momentarily interested, "it's a part of nature."

"I know that Lil. I told you that. Don't you go start telling me things I already know. 'Specially things I told you or you wouldn't even know nothing about them." Luther was annoyed and to punctuate it, he picked up his pace.

"You're the one who said the tree was gonna be mine."

"I know that too. Now are you gonna shut up and listen or you gonna keep running that mouth of yours. Good Lord Jesus! I know for sure you my child. Ain't nobody in this world talk more than me, but you coming on up there." His anger brief, he trudged on.

"God give me this gift. Nature delivered it to me. Me. Lillian you understand that. Me." he said, pounding his chest. "That tree is mine. Nobody else has seen it, nobody else can see it except you and me. And I showed you where it was."

"I know that." Lillian said.

"It's mine. That's all I'm saying. And when I'm gone. It will be yours." Suddenly Luther stops frozen. His right hand shoots up to warn Lillian. His eyes are now closed. His face grimaces. Lillian watches as he eyelids flutter. She is frightened, as she is every year. She thinks momentarily about running away, something she has always wanted to do when it happens. She stares at him, waiting for a sign.

Everything around them is quiet and still. Luther then erupts with a shout,

"No. It is not. I don't believe you." Then drops to his knees.

"Are you okay?" Lillian is ashen with fear. Luther's face is blank, as if he had left his body and in that time it had ceased to function. He looked as if he had lost time, as if he had accelerated his life. When he opened his eyes he looked at her and said, "We're not far, are we?"

Lillian smiled at him, knowing everything was all right, "No, it's not far at all."

"It's still there Lillian. I know it."

Her memory painted his face across her mind. Now completely recovered, she smiled. It was the first smile of the day. It was October first.

As the sun perched itself upon its mid-day throne, Lillian steeled herself for her coming ordeal. Every year it was the same; the same memories, the same doubt.

Her life accommodated her promise to Luther. She knew that no matter where she wanted to be or where she was, on October First she had to be in Northfield. She had worked for a year as a waitress at a downtown Minneapolis restaurant after high school. In that world she carried food to people who ignored her. She could have been a pack mule. It was here that she was forced to face the truth of her destiny. She craved understanding. She was different. It wasn't her fault. She decided then to enroll at the University of Minnesota.

Thin threads unraveled from time marked her knowledge of Luther. Lillian wanted to know more about him. From the brief moments on Christmas Eve when he watched with gleaming eyes as she opened her gifts, to the long traumatic walks on that one October day each year, she had only the vaguest impression of who he was.

Her mother never talked about him. If Lillian asked her directly, she would receive a cold stare, an admonishing and final "Don't ask me about him." It was unfair Lillian thought, but her mother was stubborn, unbudging in her will.

In the tenth year of the trek to the butterfly tree, Luther was obviously tired and weak. He spoke differently than ever before. After they had reached the tree and were returning, he told her the specifics of his visions. It was the last time they talked.

Those first ten years when Luther accompanied Lillian through the wooded area to rest underneath the butterfly tree were bathed in soft blue lights. She would lay in his arms as he told her stories and made jokes. He would explain himself to her. Although she was young, she remembered him trying to tell her why people thought him so strange.

Later, at sixteen, long after Luther was shot in a bar in Chicago, Lillian went out with a young man who had grown up in the same neighborhood that Luther had. It seemed that Luther was legend there.

They were watching a movie, when Lillian tried to explain her opinion about its meaning. Her attempt came near the end of a scene the young man was particularly interested in and he turned to her abruptly, saying:

"C'mon sugar, don't lutherbrown me now please. I want to hear this part."

Lillian was struck stiff, her mouth open, her breath empty. "What did you say?"

"I'm trying to hear."

"No. I mean what did you say about Luther Brown?"

"Oh. That's just an expression," the young man said as he uncomfortably divided his attention.

Lillian was still stunned. "Luther Brown" is an expression?"

"Yes Lillian. I don't know where it came from actually. There was this guy who used to live in the neighborhood. He's the one that started it. Now can we watch the movie."

As they walked to the car Lillian brought it up again. "You grew up on the Northside?"

The young man looked at her, "Yes."

"What does Luther Brown mean?"

"Are you still thinking about that. Well to lutherbrown somebody is when you start giving somebody all your opinions about something when the person you're talking to is preoccupied with something else. Everybody over North knows that." The young man was too smug to explain anything to. Lillian asked him to take her home.

It seemed now that the birds had grown quiet. She slowed her pace. The woods were thickest here. She knew this path, had walked it many times in her sleep. She had either been carried or walked it twenty two years running.

She heard a rustling of leaves in her head. Her hands instinctively reached toward her head, as if to hold it on.

"Back again? I thought for sure you wouldn't return after last year." Lillian flinched, closed her eyes trying to blot it out. "I declare. I am surprised. Where you going?"

"But I told you last year and year about that, it ain't out here no more."

"And you know as well as I that I've still got to find it." Lillian opened her eyes and held her head up. She focused on Luther, or perhaps a vision of him.

"You're wasting your time," Luther chuckled. "Last year I was just joking. Just like every year for the past ten, twelve years, I've been joking. Just passing time. But this year," He cut a sly grin, his eyes throwing off a near blinding glint, "this year it's for real. Chopped it down myself."

"You did not. Don't lie to me." Lillian tried to remain calm.

"Destroyed it. What's one tree anyway?" Luther produced his handkerchief and wiped his mouth. "You're crazy anyway, coming all the way out here, in the middle of nowhere just to see a stupid tree. Especially a tree that don't exist anymore."

"Then why are you here?" Lillian pressed him.

"I'm here because I knew you'd come. I wanted to bring you the news. The butterfly tree is no more."

"I don't believe you."

"It's true. Would I lie to you? Go home Lil. This is a waste of time. You can't keep going like this. Year after year. Anyway, the tree is gone."

"You told me Daddy. Don't you remember? I know it's still there."

"You're crazy Lillian. Have you bought a black derby yet? Some red pants maybe?" Luther sat down on a downed tree trunk.

"Maybe. But I promised. I'm here."

"There is no tree."

"I don't believe you."

Luther's teeth now showed fully. His cracked lips spread to accomodate his broad grin. Lillian stared at him, fighting within herself. She wanted to run to him. She tried not to blink her eyes. She tried.

In the instant that they closed Luther was gone. Lillian let her arms fall down limply to her side. She leaned on a wide oak tree standing next to her. Again the tears found their freedom.

Lillian flashed immediately upon their last walk together. It was at that time that he made her promise to continue the annual ritual. For the past three years he had been leading up to it. Telling her how important it was. Telling her that she could never survive without making the hike each and every year. Then in the tenth year he finally made it clear to her. There really was no one else. She was the only one. She had to promise.

"Lillian?" She remembered him saying.

"Yes?"

"Do you know how to keep a big secret?"

"Yes daddy."

"You're a pretty smart little girl Lil. People will always try to put you down you know, but you're pretty damn smart. I can tell. Don't pay no attention to them. You hear?"

Lillian remembered being nervous, sensing something important was going on.

"I know you probably think I'm a little strange too." Luther continued.

"No I don't."

"I hope not sweetheart. But folks try to take your free will away. They try to make you be just like them. I've seen it. But let me tell you something. You know why we got to get to this tree each year?" Luther looked up at the butterfly world barely moving above him.

Lillian had been waiting for years to know.

"The year before you was born I came through here by accident. My car broke down about five miles down the road. It was a beautiful fall Sunday morning. I cut through this here path trying to make up some time. Thought it was a short cut. Well, I almost walked right by here without seeing it. Then, bam. I looked up and Lord have mercy I see this tree standing here full of butterflies. They was barely moving.

"They looked at me and I looked at them. Their wings hardly moved. Before I knew anything I was sitting over there on that stump, just staring at this tree with butterflies all over it. Just like it is now. I must of stayed like that for three hours. Lost all track of time."

He appeared totally at peace. Lillian now felt transported into some envelope of super existence.

"We could have been butterflies Lil. We could be up there, orange and black, perfectly shaped. We could be up there just watching everything pass us by. The truth is that those butterflies up there is us. You and me Lil. Not everybody. Just some of us. Me. I'm definitely one of them. I raised you to be one too."

"I'm not no butterfly,'" Lillian said to him as she turned away from him and stared at the tree. She could see the gentle flutter of the butterflies as they staved off a gust of wind pushing in from the north.

"Every year they tell me that I've got to come back. Can't let them down Lil. They won't protect me if I don't. Can't survive without them, just can't do it. But this year they telling me I've got to make you promise Lil. You got to promise yourself to them too." Luther was beyond her. She took his hand to make sure he was still her father. To see if it felt the same. It did.

"To who?"

"To the butterflies. Nobody else knows where they are. Nobody else can reach them and understand the purpose."

Lillian's hesitation vanished. She wanted to please Luther. "Okay. I promise."

Luther's face exploded in happiness. He bend down and kissed her forehead. "Baby now listen to me. What you got to do is come back here the same day, today, October first, every year you are alive."

"Okay," Lillian said, "I like to come here."

Luther frowned. "No Lil. When you come back without me you won't like it."

"How come?"

"Because then it will be yours." Luther pulled her to him. She could feel him breathing hard. She became afraid. His calm voice was masking a heaving chest. "Try to understand baby. You know how when we're out here I get those ah .. those blackouts ... when I sort of just fade out?"

"Yes."

"I see my father Lil. He's sits right over there sometimes. And he tries to make fun of me and scare me and chase me away."

"But your father is dead isn't he?"

"I don't know anymore Lil. I see him."

"Why does he try to scare you away?"

"At first I didn't understand it. I thought I was crazy or something, but after a bit, I realized that to see it, to experience this beauty," he said pointing to the tree, "I had to face him. I had to deny even his will."

"And after I'm gone and this tree of dreams is yours," he continued, "You'll have to deny mine."

Luther stopped, stared in silence for long painful minutes. Lillian watched him, struggling with his shadow. When he turned back toward her there were tears streaming down his dark brown cheeks.

Lillian was transfixed. Red pants. Black derby. Tears flowing. Large man. Face in brown, full cheeks, small holes where the whiskers would be tomorrow. Large brown eyes. Like oversized marbles. Luther looked at her.

"For you Lil. For you and me and those of us who cannot be here. Dreams Lil. Each butterfly is a dream for us. When there is no life ahead. When we are forced to become empty bodies moved by the spirits of others, we must find the butterflies. They wait for us. We must never dissappoint them. This is where we must come."

Yes. So here she was. Haunted in the woods like a character in a movie. She neared the place where the tree was. She thought for just a moment that perhaps the tree had been cut down. Maybe everything would change. With no tree there would be no butterflies, no need to keep a promise. But no, she reasoned, the tree was there. It had been given to her to safeguard. Dreams were there.

Again she was struck stiff as Luther emerged out of the bushes and walked toward her. This time he was not smiling. His derby was badly encrusted with dirt and blood. His clothes were shredded. There was a deep cut on his right arm and an obvious knife wound on his stomach. He appeared to be stunned. His mouth moved but no sound was made.

Lillian closed her eyes tight. This vision she wanted to go away. When she opened her eyes again Luther stood within an arm reach of her. The blood was real. He was hurt. She reached to grab him. He stepped back.

He moaned as he found voice again. Lillian stopped. He held his left arm up to ward her off, "I don't have much time," he said. "I come to warn you. You can't come here anymore. Forget your promise. There isn't a butterfly tree. Never was."

"Yes there was. Every year you brought me here. Even before I knew what you were doing. Even before I could walk, when I was just a baby, you brought me here to see it."

"I created it Lil. It's not really there." Luther slumped down by the side of a tree, his life clearly receding.

Lillian stared at his body. Again the woods were quiet. "I come here every year. Just like I promised," Lillian began, holding back a new wave of water. "You told me it would be hard. But I promised and I keep coming back. But, daddy, I swear I don't understand. Why are you doing this to me?"

"Because the whole thing is a lie. You hear me? A lie. Never was no god-damned butterfly tree." Luther faded.

"There was too. I saw it. I was there. I'm here. It's right over there." Luther slid to the ground, his chest motionless.

Lillian, now screaming, "I don't believe you. I'm sorry, I just don't believe you. It is there." She turned to find it. After two steps she spotted it: a wide and regal oak tree with a short strong trunk. It appeared to be at the peak of its season. If one did not know, it would be easy to mistake this tree for any other tree. But as Lillian looked close, she saw the butterflies. Hundreds of them, clustered about the tree, lining the branches like dead leaves. As if each leaf held within itself a life. Aside from an occasional flitting about, the butterflies held themselves still.

Their colors mesmerized Lillian as they always did. The blackness of the border outlining their wings held perfect contrast to the oranges, yellows and reds which flowed along the wings and on to the body. With the slow movement of their wings, as they stood quietly, holding on to the tree, there seemed to be a unified heartbeat that Lillian felt. She turned back to Luther. He was gone.

She turned back to the tree, moving toward it. For just an instant she wanted to find a rock and toss it up at the butterflies who were staring at her.

"You go to great lengths to keep me away. Why do you make it so hard? Every year I live to find myself greater, to find something within myself which stimulates me, challenges me. That is what my father wanted for me. You are that to me. But why do you try to scare me, turn me away. You make my burden that much heavier.

"Yet you just sit there, a new bunch every year, waiting for me. And you look prettier each year. So wonderful. I know what he saw in you. I know what you are. Without you there would be no visions. And each year you push me into a new world. But does it have to be so painful? How can so much beauty bring such acute pain?"

She sat down on the grass, ten feet away from the tree, and watched the butterflies. She was exhausted. She lay her head back against a fallen tree trunk and closed her eyes. It was peaceful now.

FOR GYANNI

Alexs D. Pate

once she was a smile
a warm light
on a glass like body
of water

she rose and fell
with the moon
holding forth the land
as it slid in and out

in a world so illusory
that children only dance there
i sometimes seek her for comfort
to touch as fathers do
on rainy days
when outside charms are like
acid

down the street she'd bound
as i turned the corner
hot sticky city streets
awash in her colors
wet with her
and her friends
would stare as we
clutched our lives

she promised herself to me
as forever and
to her my heart shuddered
pledging the world
as her future

our feet grew roots
in the cement
curling into the
crevices

we transformed to beasts
and roamed this new land
where fathers and daughters
know beauteous light
hold it tightly
as her face wore
the sparkle of hope
beaming stars

then she was gone
perhaps on a search
for me
with sadness tacked
to her body

so enshrouded
she gripped my heart
as if to strangle

i reached out
screaming my need to know
and she learned
what promises are
when they shatter

FULL MOON OVER MOUNT DIABLO

Alexs D. Pate

it is night and the moutain roads
wind up toward heaven
tattered shacks lodge swatches of men
standing in lines
drinking, passing time

goats stumble about the road's shoulder
not bleating, barely breathing
as the hot jamaican air swirls
on the way up mt. diablo

the country beneath us creaks
on rough roads traveled by spain
and in the night fires shimmering
across the hillside
in the billows of ganga burning
in the sweet pungent aroma
of chicken cooking on the spit
it can be felt bubbling down low

the english have also touched heart here
as below in the twinkling lights
the country suffers dryness
and though old dark faces crinkle
showing cracked, yellow teeth,
nothing good comes of it

africa came here to rest
settling like dust upon the sugar cane
yet the wind does move it
casting it forth into soft eyes
facing life in a sweet dread

underneath all marks fade
and frozen chaos churns,

this road to kingston is confused
bewildered/anxious

jamaicans live through pictures
of themselves/feel themselves being
swallowed/being eaten/feel themselves
torn asunder

the moon is full over diablo
between kingston and ocho rios
up there in mounds of bauxite
well beyond the hopes of a people

NOTHING CHANGES

Alexs D. Pate

candy kisses
they throw
like silver dollars
clanging to the floor

i thought that shadow
was my only way of life
but no,
it goes on
like the Temptations

A LATE NIGHT MESSAGE TO OWEN
(To Owen Dodson)

Alexs D. Pate

for a moment in the mist of manhattan
we shared history/became the fire of the night
amongst the treasures and cognac
we sniffed the realms of poetic peaks
as you reached through infirmity
to a richness

you laughed and made eyes at the women
demanded attention
made poetry alright with your
characters from the streets and city lights
you hung oriental lanterns across broadway
and proclaimed love is what arose

smelling as sweet as soft
as an old man who'd created new worlds/
spun gold, dreamed of opera/
a new creation undiscovered/
it sings
in your space/on the streets
in the colors
marking the spot where love and art
convulsed in union.

INSIDE TRASH

Alexs D. Pate

for you i crept inside,
knelt in the darkness,
waited until they were gone;
stealthily unhinged their reality,
reached in
filled my pockets with dreams
and shiny things.

sometime last night
they found out
the stars were fired up
like tiny furnaces
dispatched were hunters,
marksmen, archers,
giants all.

blood hounds lurched forward
smelling me
everyone smells me
i leave a trail
and the dreams i stole
and the shiny things
leave traces in the sand
under my feet.

i stole them for you
to express my discontent
to show how much
i disdain their wealth
and how much i know you need it.

they control this world
big machines which create stuff,
shiny things and long fancy dreams;

their rules are unfair
hold you underfoot
make you wrong, alien.

and i love you.
i thought it should be done;
their shiny things are only so big,
can be carried great distances,
i wanted you to have them.
to touch them once.

but the truth must be said
they poisoned me
trapped me with their dreams
i only thought you wanted them
because i did.

the archers now draw their bows
the points of their arrows stare
eighty foot giants lined
in rows of ten,
for one who stole dreams and shiny things.

my words are like gushing blood
which stains the boots of giants
as they release their punishment;
and in gasp of love, i speak:

"it is curious, this bond
between dreams and shiny things."

DETENTE TODAY

Alexs D. Pate

detente madness absolute
undeterred, fixed wing
flown bird dying
crushed velvet
burning bushes of
hushed starlings
crippled oil slickened feathers
no movement
pointed noses
angular features
nobility pushed aside
curses upstage
and 'round back
twigs piled 2 feet
as fire wood
surrounding
dead bodies fucking
amidst smoldering
squirrels;
fossils of the future
detente tomorrow
if not today

IN PREPARATION FOR FALLING

Alexs D. Pate

falling
is something i can see before me
a place below where the lights shimmer
express no hope, hate no hearts
/live in emptiness
there at the bottom
where i have no family

where i have nothing
where we all say it in whispers
that ring like the rocks
from an ice age
falling folly
chapters unread
with yellow pages
crumbling

falling
like water dripping
from a faucet in a vacant house
like a balloon pressed for time
falling in a speed which whirls and
creates noise
as babies crying in the night

falling hopes
epithets unwound
/recoiled anger in waiting,
a gentle breeze on an open wound
stinging, unbridled pain
falling

twisting in the dead air
searching   reaching   flailing
arms flapping
seeking handles in the dark

as lost words tremble out
and are gone
/lost behind me

falling
this is
falling

POETRY READING IN MINNESOTA

Alexs D. Pate

i   swear
i come
to these things
thinkin
i'm gon learn
somethin

peoples
be talkin
all hushed like
til that girl get to
citin

all a sudden
sweat be easin out
an you get to flyin
or walking in the woods
lookin at leaves an
wishin you was smoke
blowin on away

trash talkin dey call it
back where i was,
here folks pays money
an makes cheap whispers
in dusty room corners
till it be over

A MESSAGE WRITTEN IN SOAP
AND FOUND ON A MIRROR
IN THE BATHROOM

Alexs D. Pate

before me tonight
a bowl of cold soup
an overdue bill
electric
an overflowing ash tray
a pipe half empty
a warm can of beer
unopened
New Black Voices
scotch tape
broken crackers
Banking Magazine
a shadeless lamp
shining
salt shaker
business card
forty cents
kraft barbeque sauce
wheat joint papers
and manuscripts
a nude black woman
and cookies
all surrounding
a typewriter
electric

HAVE YOU NEVER BEEN EXPERIENCED
(for James Marshall Hendrix)

Alexs D. Pate

squirming in mud
nearly destroyed
cute electric shocks
swear from your pelvis
(remember elvis)
thighs spread
liquid joy on fire
molten black
chocolate sex dripping
running
creeping
thru manic depression
bold as darkness
love squints/
     angels
laugh down
as gods make love
on war
hendrix must grimace
and dissappear
third stone
thrown from a sun
saboteur
music delays reward
little wing is a whore
guitars are frenetic lovers
masochists?:
     "whup me baby
     whup me baby"
draw the heat
work out
on a voodoo chile
heave nuts til we stone free/

each glint shatters a drum
each drop a sparkle
deafens and stills
hendrix cried Mary
the wind ...
(if 6 was 9/ 69 would be heavy)
                    ... the wind
was bare shouldered
transvestite sans rouge
as the memory drifts up
through pink nostrils
glamour coated
blending into bleeding
guitar picks
as yesterday's child
has gone and
been dead nearly a decade

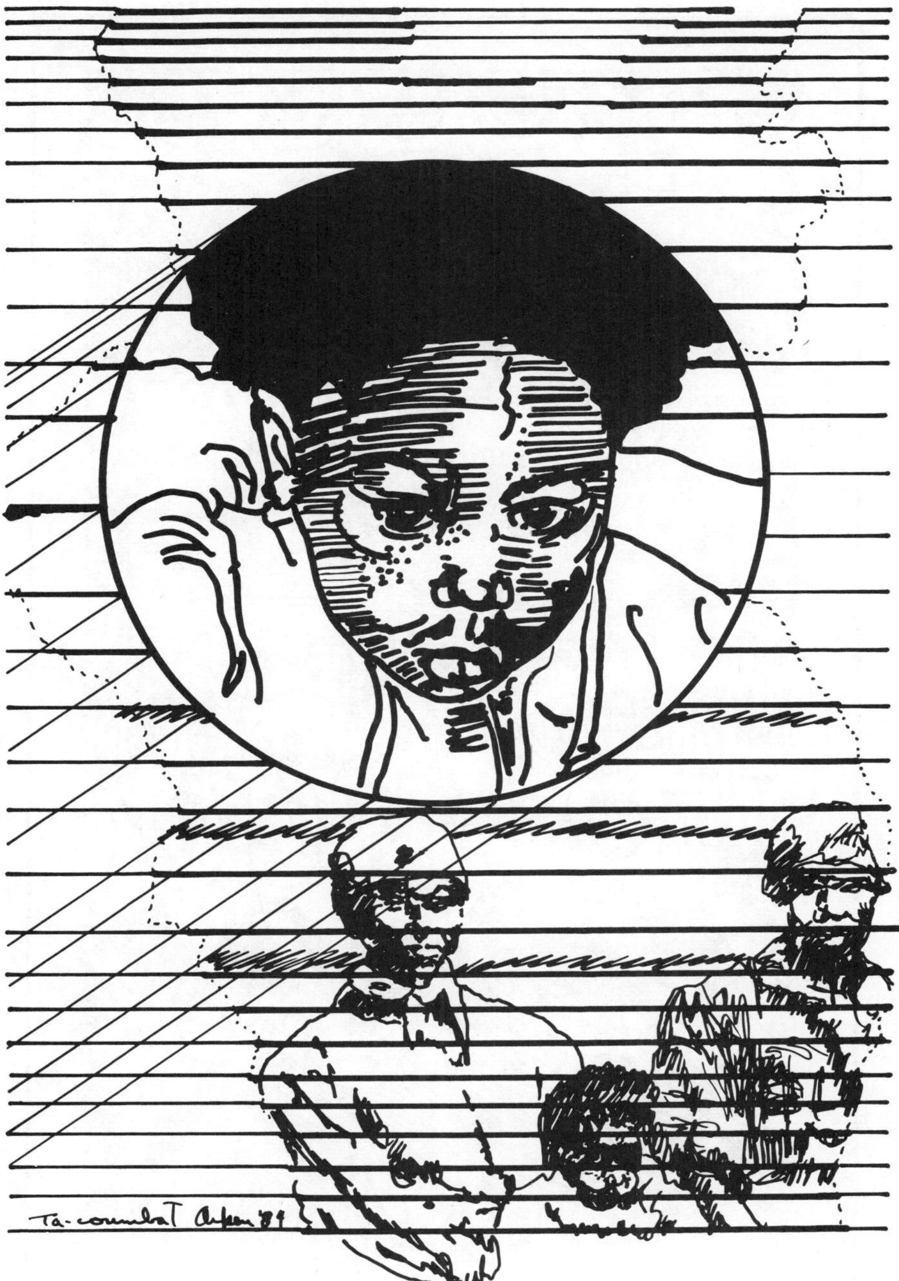

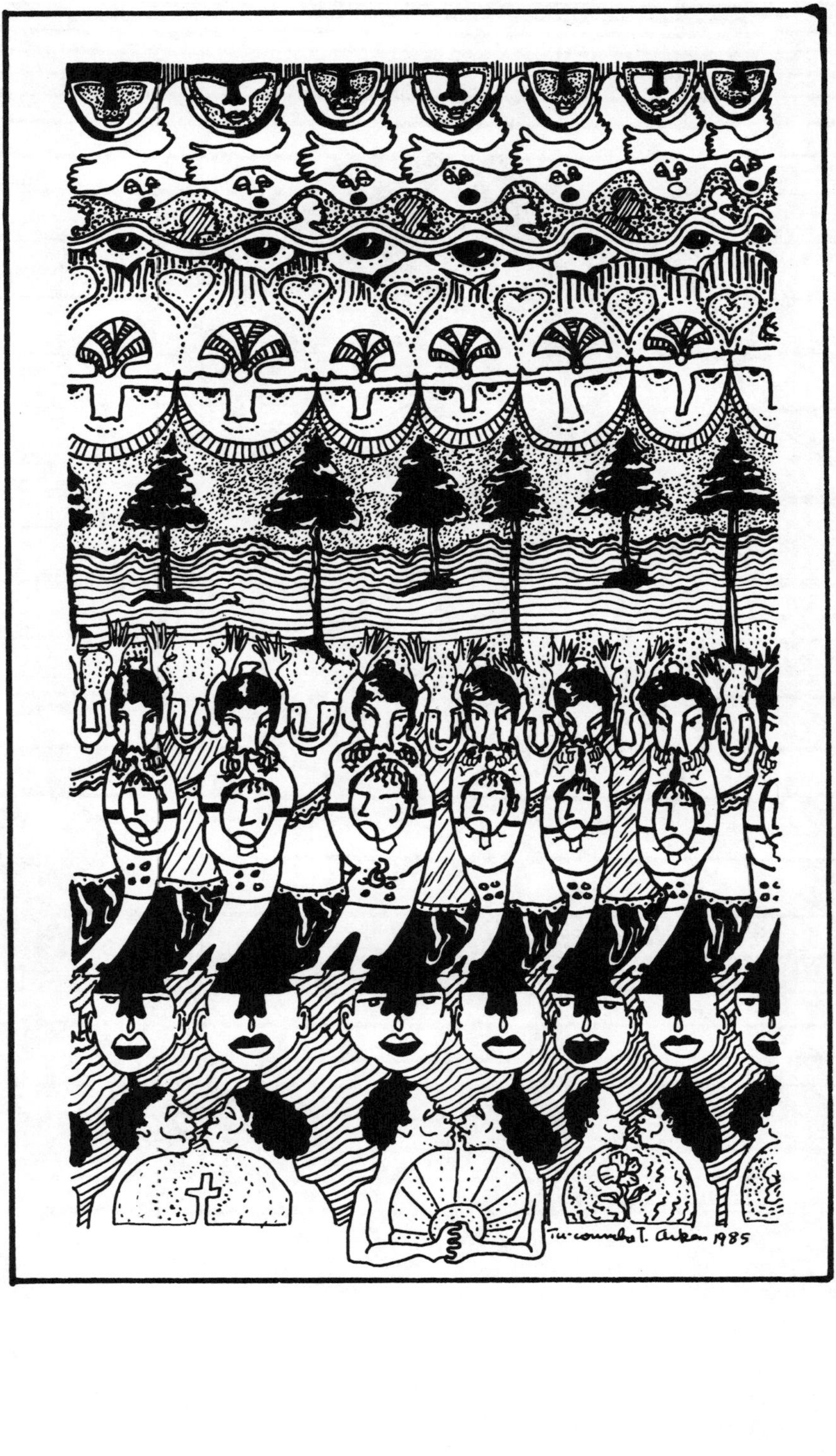
1985

BLACK FOLKS AND TRAINS

R. F. Gillum

"Black folks and trains goes way back,"
the old man said, "yessuh, way back.
We ain't had no truck with aeroplanes."
He had never flown and never would,
he assured me, wrinkled hands resting
on his cane, shifting a wad of tobacco
beneath his lower lip. His few yellow
teeth showed in a knowing grin.
"My granddaddy was a runaway
slave, nailed up in a big box
and shipped up to Philadelphia
on the train. He settled thereabouts,
got married and raised my daddy
and his brothers and sisters.
My daddy laid rails for the Pennsylvania
line most 'til he died. I got
me a job as sleepin' car porter back
in nineteen and twenty-two. I was
glad to get it even tho' the railroad
treated us pretty bad and some
white folks would wear you out and then
not even give you a decent tip.
I was there when A. Phillip Randolph
came on as a new porter but soon
got fired for speakin' up and trying
to organize us a union. He kept on though
and we finally did get us that union
even tho' many of us was fired in the process.
Me, I spent fifty years riding them rails
between Philly and Chicago. Fed me
my wife and five kids too. Yessuh,
us black folks and trains goes way back."

OUR TIME, OUR SONG

R. F. Gillum

"... the present —
a great conglomeration of noises and analogous
to the strident impression of a fast express
(the 20th Century Limited) rushing by.
The rhythm is jazz."

—Hart Crane

Near the Gambias mouth,
a pregnant tortoise is
swallowed by a shark,
carried to new continents;
she cleaves with crushing jaws
the dying dark belly to
claim new kingdoms
for her children.

Aesop and Remus balance tales.
High John and Henry tip the scales
from antiquity, bring a people toward
its century. An eagle bites
the serpent in two. Swallowed whole
Brer Rabbit wriggles free before
the squirming ends reunite

A black man climbs from a
Cleveland cellar. No longer forlorn
he takes his tambourine and plays
for the carcass floating on the sea;
somewhere there may still be someone
who has not heard his song.

Black and glistening on its rails
this locomotive culture impales
its conqueror. Attuned to
the commotion of the soul,
preferring flesh to steel,
it sings the century,
what it is and what it is to be.

JENNINGS' ACRES

R. F. Gillum

Flies buzzed seeking the cool inside
As we went out into the old man's garden.
He sat down upon a shaky stool
Hands resting on his cane.
His clouded eyes brightened
As he pointed unsteadily toward
Crooked rows of cabbage,
Insect-eaten lettuce,
And tomato plants in old truck tires.
In the sweltering sun I struggled to share
His vision of green battlements in this
His last outpost of accomplishment.
Ironic that those closest to him
Did not seem to comprehend
The grim earnestness of his struggle
With hard soil and insistent worms.

BLACK PROSODY

R. F. Gillum

The rightness of rhyme
the strength of saying
the power of pictures
all agreed upon
by a consensus of ears
of the intended audience
my people and their friends
   Senghor, Diap
   Gospel and bebop

The righteous rhyme
rising out of jobless
payless pain pulsing
from the pens of new women
new men who stopped to
write, light our pages
before going finally down

    Baraka and Hughes
    Hollers and blues

The rich rhyme of
black with blue the two
resonating around the world
hurled by an uprooted
folk finding their way back.

FRESH AIR; BREATHE DEEPLY

Julie DeCosse

I have a choice.
As I run farther away
My legs gain strength.

Freedom as an alternative.
I would like
To raise my rights, with you present
Conspicuously and undeniably
against your ignorance
and insolence.
Your mouth to go in reverse
and retract your lies.
I have a choice.
Listening to you is not an
alternative.

Patterns of Life II   Tu-coumbo Tuikar '81

from LOVE AND OTHER HIGHWAYS

Pamela R. Fletcher

Chapter One
"The Going-Away Party"

The yeasty smell of leavening homemade rolls and the sweetness of baked candied yams lingered in every space in the warm house. It was alive with the noise of running water, a wooden spoon clanking against a ceramic bowl, and the accentless voice of a radio sports commentator.

On a dining room table covered with a white linen cloth sat china dinner plates, sterling tableware and crystal water glasses. A silver candelabrum holding green candles decorated the center of the table.

Standing up and bending over a rectangular kitchen table, Cleo Winfree rolled dough for a cobbler, and Belinda Winfree, sitting inches away from the edge of the table, held a large ceramic bowl of fresh, sliced peaches in her lap. She mixed in a cup of brown sugar, stirred the fruit with brisk, strong motions and watched the sugar dissolve into a sticky syrup.

Belinda glanced at her mother. Cleo's fleshy upper arms jiggled as she worked and her midriff jutted out. She wore her black hair pulled back and braided in a bulky bun, which she hadn't changed since 1934 when her 17-year-old daughter was born. The hairstyle made her plump cheeks appear fatter than they were. She would look better in a double-curl pageboy or with side bangs to cover her high forehead.

In spite of her weight and old-fashioned hairstyle, Cleo was pretty. She had skin as smooth and brown as the best brandy and deep-set, almond-shaped eyes with thick, naturally arched eyebrows. There were few lines in her face as though life had not touched her. As Belinda matured, she began to look like her mother and this made her happy because she had considered herself plain while growing up.

With her eyes cast in the bowl, she stirred the peaches and wondered if Amos would still want her once he got to college and saw all those fancy, smart girls.

"Put some white sugar in there, too." Cleo examined the mixture and then left the table to get the sugar canister. She set it on the table. Belinda continued to stir.

"Belinda?"

"Ma'am?"

"Did you hear me?"

"Did you say something, Mama?"

"Where's your mind, girl? Sometimes I swear you act like you got the mind of a bee. Stop stirring so much. I said to put some of this in there too." She pointed to the canister.

"Brown sugar, honey or molasses is better, Mama. Makes it taste richer. Wait and see how good it'll be."

"Say what? Where have you eaten it like that before?"

"Over at Frankie's. And, Mama, it's real good, too. You'll like it, honest!"

"Don't be experimenting on us. Keep it the old way, the way Big Mama made it and handed it down to me."

"Aw, Mama, that was many moons ago. We can change it a lil bit ... make it better. I bet Big Mama would like it."

"Uh huh." The woman's bottom lip protruded, making her appear like a young, spoiled girl. Her flour-dusted hands moved the container closer to Belinda. "After you put in the sugar, put in some lemon juice, a lil flavoring and some nutmeg, too, and then let it cook for a while. Oh, and add a lil butter, too."

"I know what to do," Belinda said, denting her right brow and looking at the can of sugar. She watched Cleo pick up the dough and then stretch and pat it into a deep roasting pan.

"You know your daddy. If it tastes a teeny bit different, we'll hear his mouth from now til the Good Lord knows when. 'What ya'll do to the cobbler. Shit, I should have made it ma damn self.'" She giggled, looking at her daughter's serious face.

"Go on, baby. Finish the peaches, now. They'll be here directly."

Cleo went to the sink, carrying a gummy bowl full of utensils. While washing them, she watched Matti Bell Thompson through the window. She was stepping inside her house with grocery bags.

While Cleo stood at the sink with her back turned, Belinda added more brown sugar to the peaches. In addition to the nutmeg her mother told her to add, she sprinkled in ginger, cinnamon and cloves, which she had taken from a small bag. She then transferred the fruit to a cast-iron Dutch oven and sat it on the stove to cook. Belinda cleared the table, carried the sugar canister back to its place and began to shelve the spices in the cupboard.

Cleo faced her, smiling.

"Matti Bell's coming by for a minute. She's such a nice girl to come and stay with her Auntie Benny. Maybe you'll get to know each other better. Benny say she's so lonely ... what's this?" She picked up the can of ginger.

"It says 'ginger', ma'am."

"Don't be flippant, Belinda Jean. You know what I mean. Did you use this? And this and this?" She reached for the cans of cinnamon and cloves. "Where did these come from?" She frowned at Belinda, holding up one of the cans.

"I bought them today when I went to the store with Daddy—."

"Didn't I say to leave it as it is? You can change it when you have your own kitchen. This is my kitchen and there's going to be only one woman in it!"

"Mama, I'm making this cobbler, too. I didn't tell you what to put in the crust, even though I have a new recipe for crust, too. Why can't you try new things?"

94

"Don't try to change things around here just because you think they're not good enough anymore. Wait til you get your own house."

"I ain't never gon' have my own kitchen!"

"I'm afraid you won't if you keep talking like that. Amos won't want a woman talking like she's from the back woods of Texas."

"Mama, you know he's going away to Morehouse and I just know he'll marry one of them fancy, smart Spellman girls. That's what Junior did. That's what they all do."

"Ah, so that's what's wrong with you. Can't keep your mind on anything on account of that curly-haired boy," she laughed. "Aw, girl, don't let him upset your nerves. That boy will be back. Mark my words."

"Yeah, he'll be back, all right. He'll come home to flaunt some college girl like Junior flaunted 'Miss' Catherine. Po Amelia was sooo hurt, Mama. I know it'll happen to me. Remember how 'Miss' Catherine walked down the street to meet Mrs. Gray and them? Trying to be all proper, hanging on Junior's arm, switching her ole be-hind 'til I thought it would shake aloose. And ole, crazy Junior was struttin' like he was big time ..."

She jumped up and began to mock Catherine and Junior.

"Go on, Mama, laugh. You know you want to."

"Girl, girl, girl! You have no sense a'tall. Stop that, now." Cleo smothered her laughter by covering her mouth with her hand.

"Catherine, no matter how saditty she be, is good for Junior. Your brother is such a fool, he needed a smart college woman to keep him in line."

"Then why'd you and Daddy send him to college instead of me?"

"Well, baby, I've tried to tell you before, but maybe I have to come on out and say it straight. Ernest Junior needed to go so he could have a chance to make a decent living, you see, so he could support a family. You don't have to worry about supporting a family. Your husband will take on that responsibility. Now, I know you smart. Mable told me you were the smartest in her class, even said you'd be somebody. Well, I think if you marry a good, educated man, you'll be lucky and be somebody at the same time like me." Cleo looked at Belinda as if she expected her to agree.

"Yes, ma'am." Belinda said, but she didn't agree or understand.

"Amos will be successful and he'll marry you, too. Try not to worry about it."

"But, Mama, you don't know that for sure. When we had that fight, he told me that his mama said she was glad he was leaving town so he could get away from me."

"Girl, that boy said that silly thing to spite you. He said it because he was mad. By the way, you never told your mama what happened. You wouldn't let him have his way, right?"

Belinda smiled but didn't respond.

"I know he must have said something like, 'Aw, darlin', come on. We have to do it so I won't forget you.' Right?" Cleo nodded her head. "You'll be glad you didn't. He'll never forget you now. He'll definitely come back."

95

"His hincty mama don't like me. I bet he'll find a girl who she'll like and a girl who'll let him have his way."

"He'll do what Amos wants to do because he's so darn headstrong. Besides, you treat him like he's King Solomon just like I treated your daddy. I baked many a German pound cake and cooked many a pot roast supper for that man just like I told you to do for Amos. It worked, didn't it? Men like old-fashioned ladies. And you let that boy think he's the smartest person in the whole, wide world, don't you? Even when you know better. Yes Lord," she said, staring beyond Belinda. "Your daddy's nose was wide open just like Amos'. He'll be back, baby. Besides, he won't want a woman who's been where he's been."

"You really think so, Mama? You think if I go to college, he wouldn't want me anymore? Why would he want to come back to some dumb girl? I should be going away to college tomorrow just like him."

"Belinda, look. If he goes to college and you go to college, why should he come back? You'll be no different than those stuck-up girls he'll meet. He may as well stay there and marry one of them. You're one of a kind. You're pretty and smart. You don't have to go to college to become smart. That's only book smart, anyway. There's plenty of educated fools out there. I'd rather have an uneducated daughter than an educated fool. Now, get out of here. That boy will be here directly."

Wearing a bathrobe, Belinda trudged from room to room. She began her journey from the kitchen, constantly opening the refrigerator door, doing nothing but glancing inside, and "just wasting valuable time," according to her irritated mother. Cleo ordered her to get dressed.

Belinda moved to the sofa in the living room and listened to the baseball game for a few minutes. She then went to the bathroom for the fifth time in forty-five minutues. Although she felt a persistent urge, she didn't have to urinate. It happened that way when she felt anxious. Finally, she ended up in her bedroom.

She didn't want to see Amos that day or any day. She wanted him to leave so she could begin to forget him. Regardless of what her mother said, she didn't believe he would come back for her.

He was going away to become the teacher that she wanted to become. Ever since Miss Calloway had told Belinda about her first teaching experience on the Navajo reservation in Arizona, Belinda wanted to go there and teach. Instead, she had to sit at home and hope for his return.

Fat-mouthed boaster. He thinks he's so damn smart. Well he ain't smarter than me. If you never come back, Amos Johnson, I won't care.

She lay on the bed and closed her wet eyes.

The door bell rang.

"Belinda, where are you, baby? Will you get that, please?"

Belinda came out of the room still dressed in her bathrobe. The door bell rang again and Cleo hurried out of the kitchen. She opened her mouth wide and gasped when she saw Belinda. Appearing as if she was about to yell, Cleo stood in silence, glaring at Belinda. The visitor pushed the bell a third time and Cleo went to the door.

"Come in, Sister Morgan. You looking mighty fine today. Where's Brother Morgan and Aaron?"

A round-shouldered, shapeless, middle-aged woman walked in and grabbed Cleo's hand.

"Teddy's out front with Brother Winfree. They talking about tomorrow's Deacons' meeting, so they sent me in here. Aaron went to pick up his date, some girl he just met. I sho hope she's colored."

"Say what, Sister Morgan?"

"Well, daughter, I know he's the only colored they got at that school right now. He spends so much time there, I can't see how he can meet a colored girl. I just hope he's not getting himself in no trouble with some white girl. He worries me so being at that school. He thinks he's so smart just cause he's in law school. White folks don't care nothing about that. I swear he's armed with fool's courage."

"Don't you worry none, Sister Morgan. Aaron's no fool. He won't mess up now. He's come too far."

"I don't know about that boy ... M m m m. Something sho smells good up in here, daughter. Smells like peach preserves. You canning today?"

"You're close, Sister Morgan. You're smelling peach cobbler," Belinda said, smiling and walking out of the hallway with outstretched arms.

"Child, you sho looking good. Get over here and give me a hug."

Approaching the woman, Belinda expected her to smell like stale bread. They squeezed and kissed each other. Sister Morgan, as sweet as overripe bananas, still smelled the same.

After Big Mama, Cleo's mother, died eight years ago, Cleo wanted her children to think of Sister Morgan as a grandmother. But, Big Mama could never be replaced, especially with some religious fanatic who kept suffering mental breakdowns. The first resulted from her learning that God's "chosen church," The Church of Christ, discriminated against its dark breathren just like the sinners of the world. Poor, sweet, ignorant Sister Morgan.

"How you been, Sister Morgan? Did you enjoy your trip? You looking well."

Belinda used to tell her that she was looking well because Cleo had told her to say it. Now she said it because she sincerely thought the woman looked sane.

"Well, a while back, I was doing poorly, but lately the merciful Lord has blessed me. I must be living right." Her eyes got brighter as she spoke.

"Belinda, what is wrong with you today? Here it is four o'clock and you still got that nasty robe on! I'm not going to tell you again, girl."

"All right, all right. I'm going now. Excuse me, Sister Morgan."

"That's all right, child. You go ahead and mind your mama."

Belinda was about to enter her bedroom when her father and Brother Morgan, a tall, blubber-bellied, middle-aged man came inside. He rushed over to her. His quick movements caused his stomach to quaver.

"Well, well, well. Getting to be as fine a woman as your mama, girl," he said breathing hard. He hugged her too tight and stroked her lower back.

She eased away from him, affixing a pleasant expression to her face.

"It's nice to see you, Brother Morgan. Enjoy your trip?"

"Yes, I must say it was good."

With a sullen face, Belinda's father watched her and she lowered her eyes.

"Excuse me, I must get dressed. I'm running late," she said, being careful not to look up.

She hurried to her room. Her mother followed her.

"Belinda, I am so ashamed," she said, closing the door behind her. "You are really acting a fool. What is wrong with you today? You better find your right mind and find it in a hurry."

"I ..."

"Shut up! Just get dressed before Amos gets here. I'm glad he and his folks didn't walk in while you stood there in that raggedy thing. This lil get-together was your idea. Now, get on the stick!"

"Yes, ma'am."

"All right. Be ready in fifteen minutes, and I mean it."

As Cleo left the room, the door bell rang. Looking out the window, Belinda saw the Johnsons' Ford parked in front of the house.

"Good evening. My, don't you look lovely in that sundress, Mildred," Belinda heard her mother say.

"I'm glad you like it, Cleo. Oh, look at this! Your table is simply beautiful, isn't it Gary?"

"Yes, yes," the man of very few words said.

The Johnsons then greeted Mr. Winfree and the Morgans.

"Mrs. Winfree, may I ask where Belinda is?" Amos said.

Listen to him talk all proper, Belinda thought.

"She's getting ready, honey. We're running a lil late this afternoon. You know how slow that girl can be. She'll be out directly. Ya'll have a seat while I get you something refreshing to drink. Hot, isn't it?"

Belinda took out dress after dress and skirt after skirt, setting them on the bed. She looked them over but didn't choose anything to put on. Her father would punish her if she wasn't ready in fifteen minutes, but she didn't care.

She heard a tapping sound at her window and opened the curtains, finding Amos standing in her mother's flower bed.

"What you doing in there?"

"Getting dressed. Didn't Mama tell you?"

"Well, hurry up and meet me at the tree."

He sat in the cool pecan tree, singing when Belinda arrived.

"Finally," he said, sounding annoyed.

He jumped out of the tree and rubbed its trunk.

"I'm going to miss this old tree. Remember when we use to play tag in it?

You were so quick, I could never catch you—you look pretty."

"I do?"

"What took you so long? Were you spending all that time getting pretty for me? Come here, let me smell you." He stretched out his arms. "You got on that perfume I gave you?"

She took his class ring off her chain and stuck the ring in his face.

"Here. I figured you'd want to take it with you. You all packed, yet?"

"Yes, and no, you figured wrong. I'm not taking it with me. You're keeping it. Why didn't you meet me yesterday at the bleachers."

"Amos, we better go in before they start to look for us."

"Why weren't you at the bleachers?"

"No reason."

"No reason, huh? Maybe I should take my ring since you've been acting so funny, Belinda."

"Here."

"No! I said to keep it."

"Make up your mind."

"I told you that I wanted you to keep it forever. Why'd you bring it out here?"

"Thought you might want to give it to your new girl."

"*What* new girl?"

"The one you'll be getting in no time flat."

"You're my girl, Belinda, *truly*. Now, put that ring back on your chain and be sweet to me."

"Why should I? You'll be writing me in a few months telling me to send it to you. Ain't it the truth? You can admit it."

> *What do you want with a bad rooster,*
> *won't crow for the dawn of day?*
> *What do you do with a bad rooster,*
> *won't crow for the dawn?*
> *What do I want with a woman like my gal*
> *won't do nothin I say?*

Someone clapped. "You sing well," Matti Bell said, approaching them.

"Oh, I was just clowning," Amos said.

"Hi, Matti Bell," Belinda said. "This is Amos. Amos, Matti Bell."

They smiled at each other.

"Your mother told me to come by. Do you know what she wants, Belinda?"

"I think she just wants you to come visit. What you been doing over there, anyway? How's your auntie?"

"She's better, thank-you. I've just been reading. I haven't been doing anything much since I've been here."

"Oh yeah? What?" Amos said.

The girls looked confused.

"I mean what are you reading?"

"Edgar Allan Poe stories."

"Ugh!" Belinda said. "Is that all you have to do?"

"He's mad, don't you think? He always writes about the strangest people, like Montresor," Amos said. "Must have been the opium."

"I don't know about that," Matti Bell said, looking bothered.

They stood in silence. Matti Bell, a petite and muscular girl, would have been attractive if she didn't have those meandering eyes. Her right eye appeared to look at them while her left eye appeared to look at something else.

"Matti Bell, have you eaten supper, yet?" Belinda said to break the silence.

"No, but I plan to cook some pinto beans and rice. I'm soaking the beans now."

"I was going to invite you to eat with us. We're having a little party for Amos. He's leaving tomorrow for college."

"Oh you are? How nice! Are you the one who goes to Texas U? Auntie Benny says your friend goes there, Belinda."

"You must be talking about Aaron," Belinda said.

"Girl, I'm not crazy! I'm leaving town for Morehouse," Amos said with a smug grin.

"Oooh! I'd like to go to Spellman but I don't think I will, though. It costs too much. I've been trying to save my money ever since my mother told me how expensive it is. I don't think I'll ever be able to save enough."

"Get a scholarship. That's what I did," Amos said.

"You did?" You must be *very* intelligent."

Belinda got tired of listening to them.

"Are you coming, Matti Bell?" she said.

"Thanks a lot, but you already have company. I'm cooking for Auntie Benny, anyway, so I better be going."

"Well, come on, Amos. They're probably waiting on us. Later, Matti Bell."

"Okay. It was nice meeting you, Amos. Good luck!"

"Thanks, Matti Bell. The same to you."

Matti Bell gazed at him and then walked away, smiling.

Belinda waited for her to go inside.

"Can't get any privacy around here," she said.

"You want privacy? Meet me at the bleachers tonight."

"Not *that* kind, Amos."

They heard a car door slam. Aaron and his date had finally arrived. When they got out of the car, Amos and Belinda waved to them.

"Sister Morgan thought he was bringing a white girl over," Belinda giggled.

"What? Why?"

"I don't know. You know how crazy she is."

"Aaron's crazy, too, but not enough to get himself lynched. It's bad enough going to school with them. But messing with a white girl, too?" They both laughed.

Facing Belinda, Amos placed his arms around her waist and brushed his face against hers.

"Hey, it's our last chance, girl. Tonight's the night."

"I told you no, and I mean it. If you don't like it, too bad—you can wait 'til tomorrow, can't you?"

"Huh? You know I'm leaving early."

"Not with me, fool. With one of them college girls."

Amos grinned. "Girl, you so evil! I'm going to start calling you 'Ole hard hearted Hannah! You don't want to send me away with blue balls, do you? I'll die!"

"Boy, get outta my face," Belinda laughed, twisting loose.

> *I'm goin to tell you somethin, baby,*
> *Ain't goin to tell you no lies.*
> *I want some that custard pie.*
> *You got to give me some of it,*
> *You got to give me some of it,*
> *You got to give me some of it,*
> *Before you give it all away.*

"You can have the whole pie when you come back, *if* you do."

"Belinda! Amos! Come on, now. We've been waiting long enough," Cleo called to them.

When they walked inside, everyone was standing around the dining room table.

"Belinda, the food is cooling off. What took ya'll so long? You should have come in with Aaron."

"Sorry, ma'am," Belinda said.

"All right now, let's all be seated," Mr. Winfree said.

Amos pulled out a chair for Belinda and then sat beside her.

"Oh, Amos, honey, you sit at the other head of the table. Tonight you're the guest of honor," Cleo said.

"Thank-you, ma'am," Amos said, standing up.

Everyone waited for him to change places.

"Will you bless the table for us this evening, Brother Morgan?" Mr. Winfree said.

"Certainly. Shall we pray. Oh, Lord, please be with our young men as they strive to do their best. Help them to achieve their goals, if it's thy will. We pray that they walk the straight and narrow path and do what's pleasing in thy sight. Thank-you, Lord, for the food we're about to receive and the bountiful blessings you have bestowed upon us. Amen."

"Amen!" Everybody said.

"This sure is nice of you, Mrs. Winfree, to cook this supper in my behalf," Amos said, watching Mr. Winfree slice the roast.

"Child, it was my baby's idea, but she left all the work to me."

"No—," Belinda began.

"Well, almost all of it," Cleo laughed.

"I helped some, but Mama's funny about others cooking in her kitchen when she's in there."

"Amen," Mr. Winfree said. "I can't stand to cook in that kitchen with her around. I say, 'honey, you go in there and have a seat. Papa's going to fix supper for you tonight.' 'All right, Ernest,' she says. 'I'm going to write Magnolia a letter.' As soon as I get the pots and pans out of the cupboard, here she comes. 'Sugar, what you fixing? Need anything? I have everything in a special place. Let me get what you need.' "

Everyone laughed as Cleo denied her husband's story.

"Mama, it's the truth, and you know it," Belinda giggled. She paused and looked across the table at Aaron's friend. "We shouldn't be carrying on so when we have a new guest this evening. Aaron, will you please introduce your date? He's too educated to have manners, you understand."

"If you and lover boy hadn't been too busy mooching over there by that big tree, you would have been in here when I introduced her earlier," Aaron said.

"Is that so?" Mr. Winfree said in a gruff voice, but then winked at his wife.

"Cora, meet my smart-mouthed play sister, Belinda and her beau, Amos."

Cora greeted them in a low voice and kept her eyes in the dish of candied yams as she spooned out a few onto her plate.

"Where did you find such a pretty young lady, Aaron?" Mr. Johnson said. Everyone looked surprised because he rarely said much, particular to strangers. His wife turned to look at him.

"Yes, Aaron, I wondered that myself," Cleo said. "I hear that you're so busy these days."

Belinda hoped her mother wouldn't say anything awful like, "You had your poor mama so worried." Then Aaron would ask why, and then the whole evening would be ruined by a discussion on the dangers of interracial dating. Even she wondered if Aaron was tempted. She knew that he felt that nothing was beyond his reach.

He looked as uncomfortable as Cora. He was a private person, which bothered his mother very much. Sister Morgan always complained to Cleo about not knowing her son. Belinda could tell that she was concentrating hard on Aaron, waiting for his answer to Mr. Johnson's question. But Aaron only smiled and commented that he loved Mrs. Winfree's homemade rolls.

"Yes, they are good, Mama," Belinda said. "But don't eat too many, ya'll. There's peach cobbler for dessert."

"Yes, ma'am! I can't wait to taste it," Sister Morgan said. "It's our favorite, ain't it, Teddy. Teddy?" She nudged him to direct his angry eyes away from Aaron.

"Yes, it is, Mae," Brother Morgan said in an annoyed tone. "Cora, did you meet my boy at school?"

Everyone was aware that Aaron was the only colored person at Texas University.

"No, she didn't meet me at school. We've been friends for a long time. Must you always pry?" Aaron said.

"Don't you disrespect me, boy!" Brother Morgan said.

"Now, Teddy, this is not the place nor the time. *Please*. Please don't do this." Sister Morgan sounded as if she might cry.

Belinda looked at her mother, who looked at her husband. Belinda prayed that her father, not her mother, would say something to cool down the situation. Cleo would say, "Aaron, don't you speak to your daddy like that. No matter how grown you get, you're still his son." Please, Daddy, please say something, Belinda thought.

"This is a very special time in our young men's lives. Let us celebrate and send them off on a good note," Mr. Winfree said. "We're here to enjoy ourselves."

"That's right, Ernest. Amos, sing one of those blues tunes you're alway singing around the house. He's always worrying me. 'Mama, listen, listen,' he says. Now's your chance for a big audience, son," Mrs. Johnson said.

"Mildred—," Mr. Johnson said.

"Oh no, it's quite all right. Go on, son," Mr. Winfree said. "We could use some entertainment."

"Yes, Amos, please do," Belinda laughed. "He was singing to me earlier."

"Aw, Mama! Why'd you put me on the spot?" Amos said. "I'm still eating."

"Go on, Amos. Just sing one, no two, sing two songs for your mother. Don't be shy."

"He's hardly shy." Belinda stood up and pulled him to his feet. "Sing the one about 'Custard pie.'"

Everyone laughed, even Brother Morgan and Aaron. Hearing them laugh seemed to cheer up Sister Morgan.

"Okay, folks. I got one especially for the womens," Amos laughed.

"Oh, oh, Ladies! Watch out!" Mr. Winfree said.

> *Sometimes you married womens*
> *I cannot understand.*
> *Sometimes you married womens*
> *I cannot understand—*
> *You serves beans to your husband,*
> *Cooks chicken for your back door man.*

"Oh Lord, you better stop right there," Cleo said, laughing along with everyone else.

"Naw, young blood. Go 'head and tell them womenfolk like it is," Brother Morgan said.

"Mildred, where'd you get such a bad boy?" Sister Morgan said.

"He came out of my womb cutting up. I haven't been able to do anything with him since."

Sister Morgan giggled. "Oh child, you so crazy."

Smiling, Belinda glanced across the table at Aaron and Cora. Cora watched Amos curiously and looked as if she didn't know what to think. Aaron seemed more at ease, being used to Amos' antics, but Belinda expected him to rush away soon after dinner. He was at his best when interacting with only one person at a time.

Four years ago, during the summer before Aaron had gone to college, he Belinda became friends. They had known each other all their lives but, because of their age difference, they had paid little attention to each other. Aaron became interested in Belinda after she began spending Saturday mornings ironing and cleaning house for his mother, who was recovering from a nervous breakdown. One Saturday afternoon, he invited Belinda to the neighborhood soda fountain. From then on, they began to frequent the place for lunch.

While he talked, she ate and watched the furrows in his forehead appear and disappear, and the crooked way he held his mouth. Aaron rarely spoke of anything but W.E.B. DuBois and the Talented Tenth philosophy. He reminded Belinda constantly of their responsibility to their race's advancement, and she envisioned them changing the world together as man and wife.

During his first semester at college, she wrote him several love letters, but received only one reply, which greeted her as "Baby Sis." By the time he came home for Christmas vacation, she was infatuated with Amos, one of her classmates.

Once again, Belinda found herself in the same situation. This time Amos was leaving her and there was no one left to furnish a new fantasy. The best young men were either spoken for or were leaving town.

No, this time she wouldn't be left behind. Tonight she would also celebrate her departure.

"Belinda, baby, will you help me serve the pie?" Cleo said.

"Of course, Mama." Belinda stood up and began to clear the table. "Amos, are you enjoying yourself this evening?"

He was now sitting and eating a third serving. Brother Morgan was standing and singing a spiritual. His wife rocked back and forth in her seat with wet eyes; her husband was singing her favorite song.

"I sure am enjoying myself," Amos said. "Everything is fine."

"Good," Belinda said. "I want this going-away party to be the best you've ever been to."

STREET WALKER

Pamela R. Fletcher

During those moments
when I've leaped outside myself,
when my wildest thoughts threaten
to bust loose and control me,
when my anger urges me to maim or kill,
I walk quickly
and allow my feet to take me where they will.

I often think I'm ugly
until I walk the streets
passing old men, young men, and boys trying to be men
calling "Hey Mama/Babee/Girl"
"Dem jeans sho fit nice/can I escort you somewhere?"
"Can I be yo friend?/ How bout an acquaintance?"
Others driving cars honk their horns
and slow down to offer me a ride.

No matter how plain my face
how raggedy my jeans
(I go to great lengths to look mean),
it doesn't matter at all.
"Hey Mama/Babee/Girl":
Infiltrating eyes
lewd grins
and blaring horns
invading my privacy.

Funny.
When I left home
I wasn't wearing my "kiss-me red" lipstick
or my fuck-me-quick hairdo
my black mini skirt
and my white, too-tight T-shirt,
looking like I want it.
Begging for it.

Maybe it's my walk
or maybe it's because I walk
aimlessly,
conveying the need for some man's direction.

But I walk to be alone
            to release my crazed energy
            and to study other women's anxious faces
while they wait at the bus stop
or trudge to their cars
as if they dread the ride home to

        helpless spouses
        horny adolescent boys
        prissy teen-age girls
        and pissy-ass babies;

as if they dread the ride home where
their wildest thoughts threaten
to bust loose and control them.

Sometimes we meet in the darkness
greeting each other
with the scraping sound of our soles.

UNTITLED

Pamela R. Fletcher

    "Drop dead," you say
    but I'm already dead
    like dry, sweet basil
    resting in a bottle,
    waiting to come alive
    in some man's stew.

I CRY THE TEARS

Pamela R. Fletcher

I cry the tears
you wanted to cry
you should have cried
day after day
while at work/upon leaving work
feeling the pain of not being seen
as just another man
as just another human being.

I am crying the tears
you should have cried
but you harbored your grief
and lived a cheerless life.
I was afraid to look into your eyes
       afraid to feel your pain
       of not being seen
       as just another man
       as just another human being.

I have cried the tears
you held inside
as you felt the way
they wanted you to feel,
as you came home
to the only place where you had some control
to the only place where you were seen
as more than just another man.
You were Father
the Rock of Gibraltar
and a fifty-degree-below farenheit day.

I cried the tears
you finally cried
as you were faced
with losing your niche
in a world you hated but tolerated.

They didn't give a damn
even after 25 years
of you biting your tongue
and swallowing your words,
shedding a layer of your manhood each day.

As they flowed
you discovered
you were stronger because of them,
you discovered
it was possible to salvage
your unraveling edges
just in time.

WOMAN/CHILD
(For Sabrina)

Pamela R. Fletcher

Woman/Child
　　at 13
　　at times
　　more grown
　　than me
　　at times
　　too aware
　　of life's realities
　　frightening me
　　with your adult insight
　　popping the pill
　　each day at three
　　only wanting security
　　whose meaning is unknown to

Man/Child
    sweet sadist
    already father of two
    some day he'll make
    a fine woman beater
    he's practicing on you
Woman/Child
    selling your heart
    to the highest bidder
    says he'll buy you
    Calvin Klein jeans
    says he'll take you
    to Valley Fair
    to the movies
    says "ooh lil mama,
    you so pretty"
    just a Woman/Child
    seeking prosperity
    finding fantasies
    unlike those
    in your daydreams
    afraid of what you'll do
    if he's untrue

WE ARE SELDOM DESIRABLE
(For all the women who are and ever were)

Pamela R. Fletcher

We are seldom desirable
once we become dull and old and worn-out
by guilt-filled clandestine affairs
with married men or younger men
     moneyed men or unmoneyed but richer men
     than our lovers/husbands
once we become broken down by
     failing marriages
     unfounded fantasies
     and passionate but hollow promises.

We are seldom desirable
once our breasts become shapeless
and crowfeet decorate our eyes
and we have wiped the last baby's bottom
and scrubbed the last tile of the kitchen floor
with dry, age-spotted hands
we try to keep moist and young-looking
with miraculous creams and lotions.

We are seldom desirable
even to ourselves
as we scrutinize our faces each night
waiting for the seventh morning
when that moisturizer will plump out our wrinkles
and those facial exercises will lift our jaws and chins.

We are seldom desirable
once our blood has become thinned with gin
or our nerves ironed out with valium
as we live in the past,
holding onto ancient hurts and amendable mistakes
we and others have made.
Can we believe that God forgives our trespasses
if we forgive our trespassers?

We are seldom desirable
we caustic bitches,
as they call us;
when they speak of beauty, grace and sage
they rarely refer to us.
We believe they are right
deep down inside
and treat our aging like Hansen's disease.

A LITTLE BOY'S HEROINE

J. G. Mentzos

Part I

There I was in shorts,
knee highs and sneakers.
Uncombed curly hair,
and large brown hypnotized eyes,
holding a flower
for the girl I watched.
While I hide in some bushes
as she searched for me ...
"Ally-ally-all-come-free!"

We would play superheroes
me and my heroine
in the morning
while the summer
sun climbed the sky.
I would always
start a fight
so she could win
and I could run home
crying, "I-hate-you-I-hate-you-I-*HATE-YOU!*"

In the evening
we would dance
to the make believe
of two children
playing house ...
she would laugh
when I cried
when she kissed
me good-bye
as I left
to my make-believe
job.

Part 2

She was a black rose
at sweet sixteen,
her skin was as smooth
as a sapphire
her eyes like
that of a night
filled with stars ...
I would follow her,
watch her
laugh
with her boyfriends,
who offered me warm beer
to go away
and play
all by myself ...
I would take the beer
with a painted smile,
so she
wouldn't know
she was
my heroine
and as soon
as I turned the corner
I would fight back tears as I emptied
the beer onto the ground.

Part 3

The necklace
I gave her on
her graduation day
was a butterfly of gold,
the secret symbol
of my heart
when I was near
to her ...
My chest was to

my heart what a field
of flowers
are to
a cocoon-freed
Monarch
when she kissed me
"thank you ..."

Part 4

We would sit
when I was older
in a dark room at
twilight
and watch car headlights
from outside
race across
the curtains.
While I sung Marvin Gaye's
songs of "I want you"
only to find her
asleep
in her chair.

Part 5

I would spend the night
with her brother
so I could sneak
in her room
when she was sleeping,
and whisper I-love-you-poems
in her ear
that I wrote
just a moment before.

Part 6

Today my heroine's a woman,
I watch her write
doodles of her lover's
name
while my heart
flutters to the ground
and dies ...

She looks at me strangely
as I walk
to the door
slowly
and say with a smile,
softly
"He'll never love you
like that
boy,
in shorts
knee highs and sneakers
uncombed curly hair
large brown hypnotized eyes.

TO LOVE A MYSTERY

J. G. Mentzos

I'm an empty thought,
                    hollow and thirsty
My thirst tastes like this (?)
          There's a silent flute in my heart,
                                   but its
music book has left me,
               and its silence
                         its embrace feels like
this (?)
      I'm a beating heart,

               for the bastard-maker,
and my throb goes like this (?) .??..?

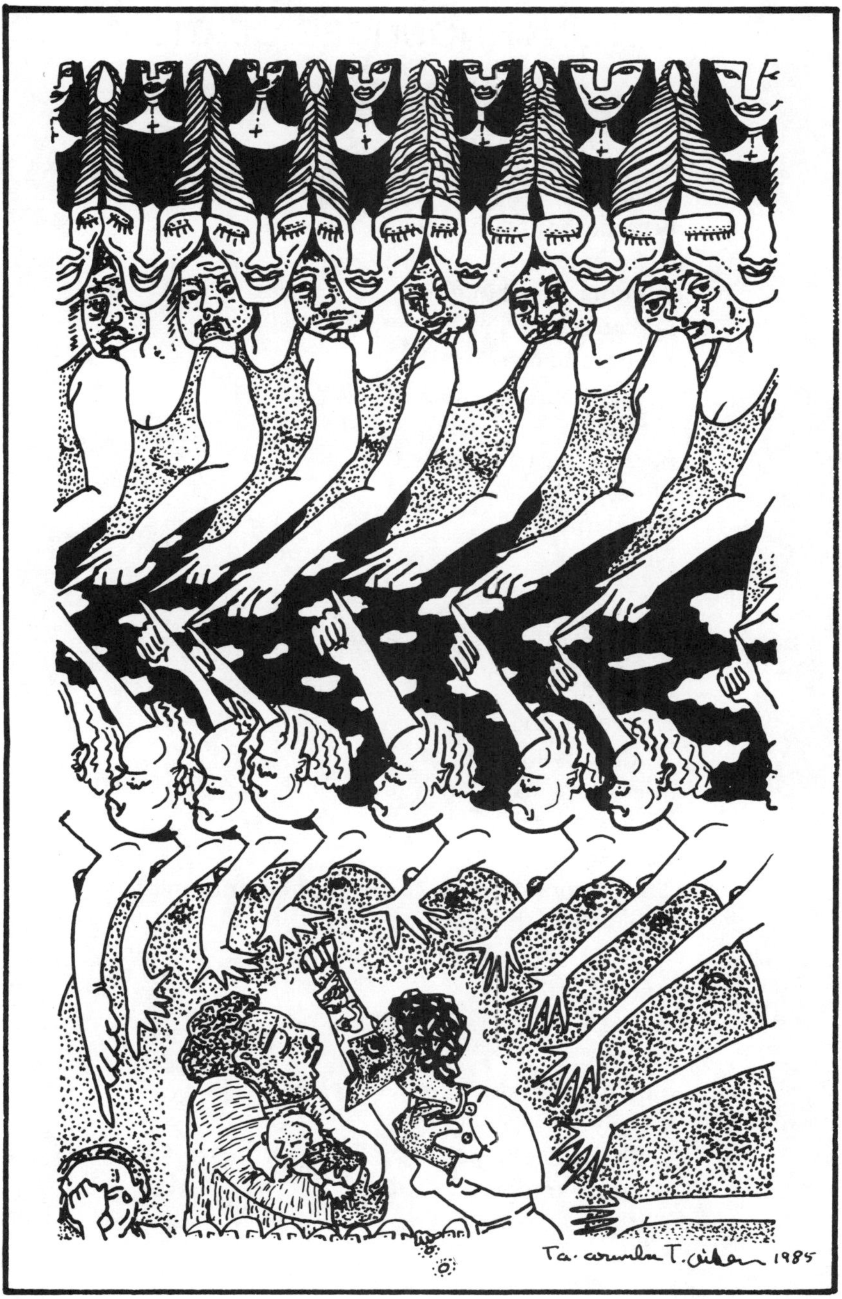

AN UNANNOUNCED DEATH

LaNette

He died
Because he lost his heart.
Abandoned,
Without forethought.
Discarded,
Along a barren road.

He died,
Because he had no soul.
No essence.
No identity.
No reason
To
Be.

He died.
Uneventfully.
Without violence.
Without a whisper.
Without a tear.
Puzzled,
That a condition he considered commonplace
Could cause his demise.

And so,
Alone,
He died.
Slowly.
Simply.
Without heavy prayers.
Without tempered songs.
Without anyone caring
He was dead.

PEACE

LaNette

There.
It was.
Without choice.
Without reason.
Disillusioned.
Fatigued.

The noise.
The screams.
The stench.
The light-
Blinding.
Now
Distant
Now
Gone.

And there it fell.
Riddled.
Motionless.
Questioning.

An unfortunate victim.
A neglected consequence.
Of a thoughtless impulse-
A deed-
Admittedly-
Not it's own.

There.
Stilled.
Tears
Dried.
Pain
Gone.

A senseless shell.

Fearful
No longer.
Void.

Filled with an empty
Endless
Nothingness
They call peace.

THE CEMETERY

LaNette

He found himself—there. Alone. Void. He inhaled slowly. Exhaled. And again. And he tried frantically to rationalize—to justify that which to him had no explanation. He was a man. And the anger swelled inside him as he felt his eyes—moist and tears—cold roll down his cheeks. He reached inside his overcoat pocket. His hand trembled as he wiped the guilt from his eyes. And he wanted nothing more at that moment—nothing—but to be dead too.

He looked out of the window. Almost dusk. Another ending. And the car moved down the narrow road while the trees stood on either side in solemn observance. He could see, in the distance, a sparse scattering of flowers in front of headstones. Slabs of masonry with curt verses.

He felt himself shivering. He pulled his coat closer. Still he shivered. And still the tears fell—singularly—one after another. He inhaled deeply and held his breath for a moment. He felt his heart pound. His body shook violently. The driver glanced in the rear mirror and without recognition stared ahead.

They made their final turn. Down the brown lane. Past the token barrier. He felt the car slow—then stop.

He saw himself standing beside the coffin. The thing—covered with flowers—soft blue-trimmed in brass. They stood there. Each face, a buried memory. Waiting for the man with God's words to speak.

She stood beside him—berating him without words. Hating him. He could see her, without looking, her face distorted with rage, clinching a sheepskin. Him—trembling—gasping for breaths.

She had found him in the city. Hiding in the darkness. And she told him that their mother was dead. She told him with vengeance. Her voice strained with contempt. Dead. She had been there with an old woman—dying slowly—asking for her beloved son. She had been there—dying too. She had been there, while he moved capriciously, through the bowels of the city. While he played low sad songs indulged in the night.

And he looked at her. Barren. His sister—bitter. His sister—lost. A man—alone. And he hated her, then and for always. A son without a mother's love.

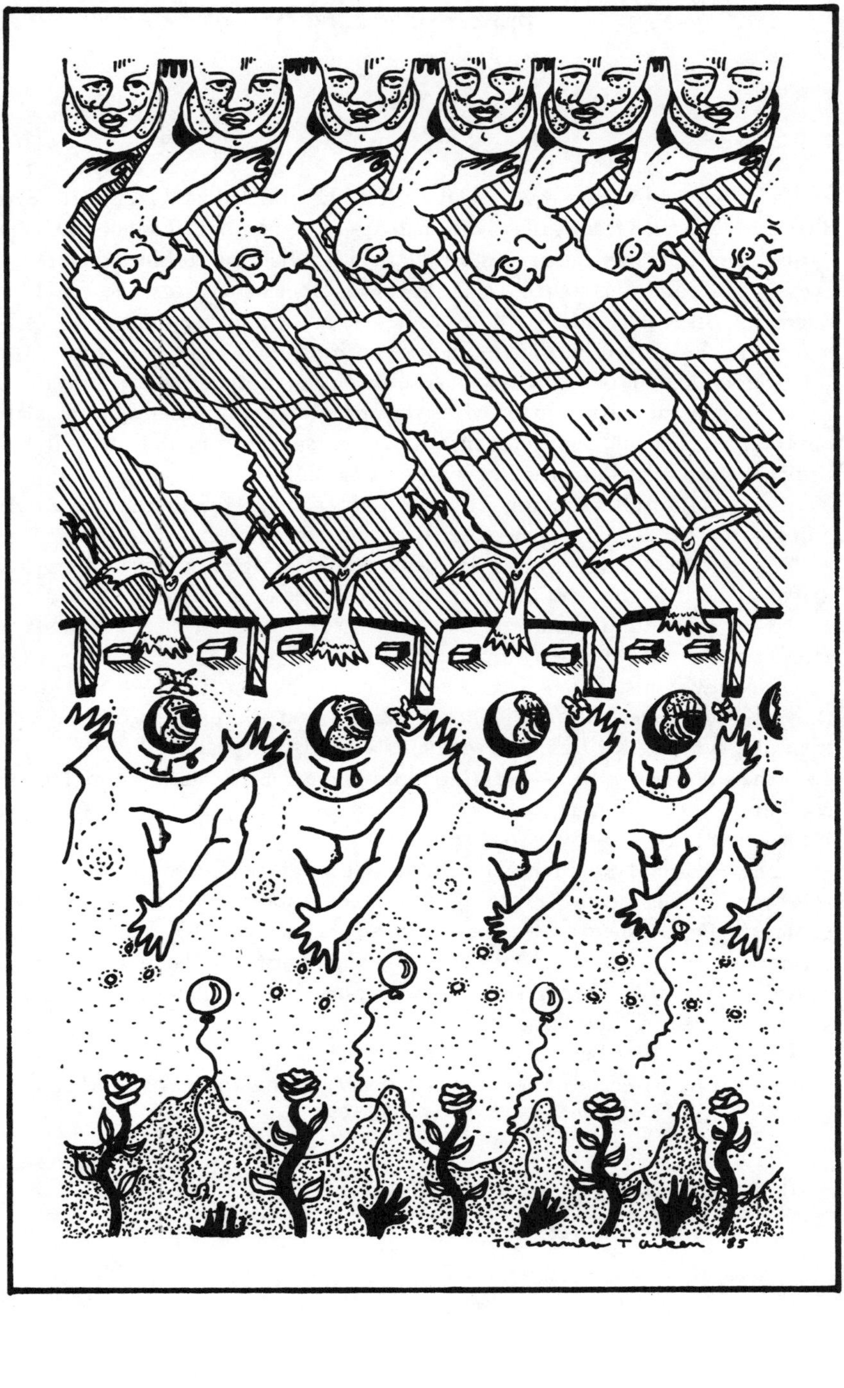

LOCATING GREIF
For Carrie Belle, Sonny & John

Roy McBride

The dying love the dead.
Dead
    the dying
        are trying.

I am driven through
the green countryside
of northern Louisiana

of northern Louisiana;
wilder than memory.
At last I will see Dodge City (Ark.)
and the mounds above the bodies
of Carrie Belle, Sonny and John.

And we cross the border
and Claudell buys his wine
and I am old enough to know
the taste
      desire
          dream and despair.
This is my family
and these are my people.

We drive through Cartwick
past the old church,
decaying beneath the creeping woods
and I walk through the mud and neglect
of the old cemetery
to stand in the rain
with memories.

John Edward.
Big John.
Big Daddy.

I remember that afternoon
we sat on the backporch on 64th Pl.,
you telling me about going to the doctor,
him telling you, "You're going to die
before you're 35 if you don't stop drinking,"
and you said,

          "We all gon' die.

          I wanna die high,"
and you cried
and I couldn't hold you in my arms
and say I love you

          We didn't

             I did

               I do

and you dried your tears
and took a drink of Gordons Gin.

Carrie Belle.
Belle.
I called
to see how you were
on Christmas day.
Mama said
you had died
that morning.
I was in Fargo, North Dakota,
on my way to Winnipeg,
on my way to Vancouver,
on my way to Seattle,
on my way to San Francisco,
on my way to Utah,
on my way to Mexico,
on my way back to you.
You were the only one that remembered
my birthday falling
four days after Christmas,
though I never remembered your birthdays,
all captured by those same four walls
on your heavy bed.

And Greyhound moved me
across icy Minnesota
and my tears were frozen
and I wanted to tell you about Mexico.

Glenn.
Sonny.
You knew there was nothing
to be done
        nothing that can be done
stoned
stunned.
Chicago is a jungle
and the animals are wild
Sonny man
       Sonny boy
          Sonny child.
And you drunk
would sit me down
and try to tell me
what it's all about,
         "It ain't worth it,
         but it's all there is.
         You know what I mean?"
I know.
I know.

My family fades,
grows old and dies,
dies young
and young, alive people
who are my family
inherit their dreams.

               (April, 1973)

MASTURBATION
For C.

Roy C. McBride

We seduce
each other
with revelations
of our dreams
and we are lonely together
friend/love
our fantasies
so often
sexual
fingers blistered
from touching
our own bodies

And we are unknown poets
wanting to know
and be knowable

And our desire
is for warm flesh
love of man
love of sky
love of windy Spanish streets
love of Paris cafes
and their memories
love of Dylan Thomas
and Wales
love
our desire is for love
and proof of it
and no one can prove
flesh pulled gently/love
spasm

And we become our dream
of flesh/love
the flesh of our desire/love
and nothing is proved/love
flesh grows cold

And we are friends/love
warmth of flesh/desire/love
understanding desire/flesh/love

roy

CHURCH OF ST. VINCENT VAN GOGH

Roy C. McBride

Nothing as simple as desire   (love)
The minister of morning sings in the light
Sun flowers
Jesus Jehovah beloved monster of pain
Worship
In all we trust / the changing light
Men turn and turn under the sun
Moving toward night / visions
Love / the flame
Your voice / my love / in the night
Your voice / my love / my ear

UNTITLED

Roy C. McBride

so glad
      this summer
            is finally over
so many tears
        &
         so much rain

got caught in a shower
got caught in a thunderstorm
got caught in a whirlwind

                got caught
                got caught
                got caught
                got caught
so glad
      this summer
            is finally over

VALENTINE
For Sherry

Roy C. McBride

You are near.
I can hear you breathing;
your footsteps growing closer.
Will you be surprised to see me?
Will you be happy to see me?
Will you see me fading into this hillside,
blending into the dusk.
I will try not to startle you
rising like a rock in your path;
falling like a tree at your feet,
flowing like the wind around you.

You are near.
I can hear your breath (quick intake-
sigh through the leaves of my soul).
I am the gentle monster inside this dragon.
Ride this flesh.
Scratch behind my ears.
I will catch your tears in my fiery throat.
Holding you near.
Calling you dear.
My heart is red and blooming.
Listen to the church bells in my chest.

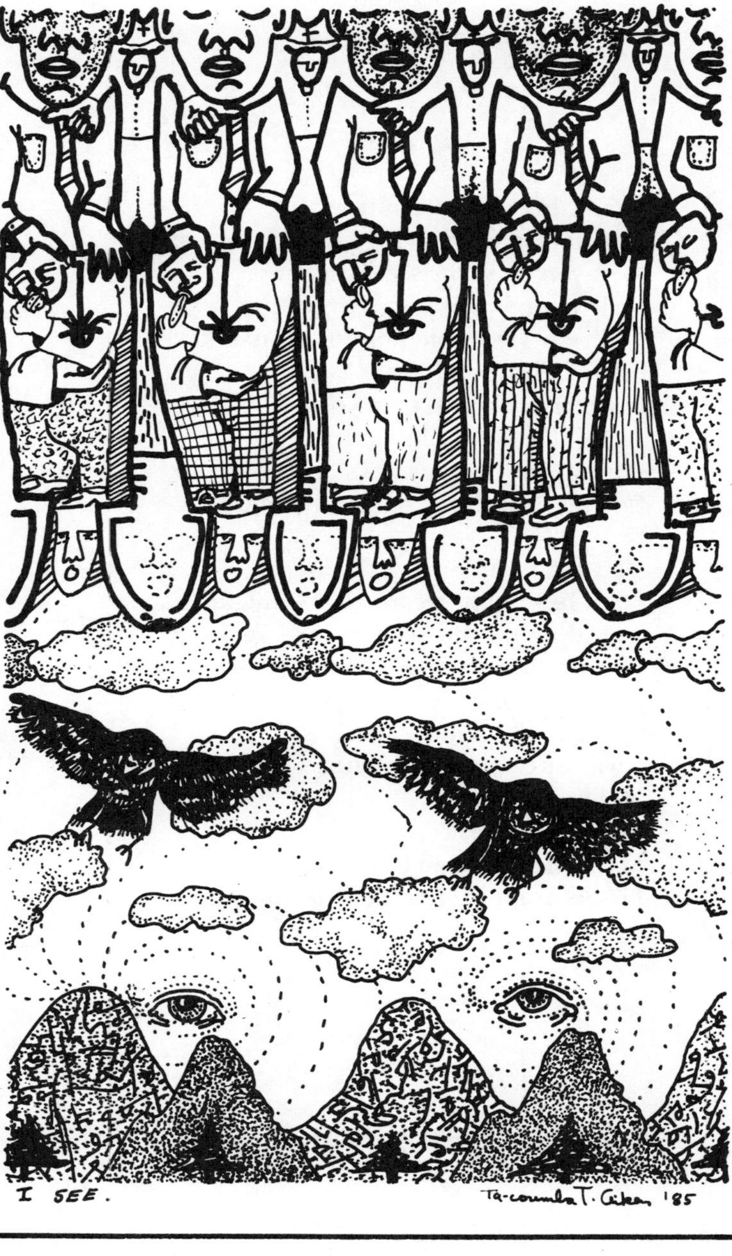

I SEE.

Ta-coumba T. Aiken '85

METAMORPHOSIS

Mary Moore Easter

One gets tired of one's own
Concerns,
Would sometimes like to trade in
The viewpoint for another.
Not opposite—too close—
But exchange it for some unknown perspective
Less logical than leaves
Changing colors,
Snakes shedding,
Moths and butterflies,
Wood to stone.

NIGHT RUN

Mary Moore Easter

The sky has come down around me
and the air, same warmth as my skin,
makes me think
that I do not end at my fingertips
or the edges of my flesh
but extend into the stars,
heart beating me upward
breath leaving
puffs of my essence
on the night air.

TIN

Mary Moore Easter

Meetings,
hurried, barricaded at both ends.
Little clumps of minutes spread out
over ten years,
sometimes counted in hours
almost never in days.

There was a time near the globe fountain
frozen in winter
you were not well
and suffering from a panic of loneliness,
asking questions, fast, unanswerable
eyes darting.
And another time
at the January Bar
where, it was whispered,
they took me for a hooker.
Still another, when walking briefly,
we saw huge teeth
in a curio window.
Meetings where numbness set in so fast
it almost swallowed anticipation.

There is no sequence,
no order in this remembrance.
I cannot name the years
and the seasons, still clear,
arrive in unnumbered lots:
two springs together,
three winters ...
And summers.
Were there ever summers?
Lake-filled and green?
And yet, we never met
—not once—
by accident.

To what does this
fragmented constancy attest?
Can it really be said
we were together a decade,
or should we ignore the lapsing of days,
add up the minutes
and call it a month in the country.

SITTING ON THE PORCH

Mary Moore Easter

An event, in those days
for which one freshened up.
The houses were close to the street
and to sit on the porch
meant to be accessible,
to visit, chat and receive,
to be public and on display.
My grandmother did not
sit on the porch
before four o'clock
but sometimes stayed there
through sweet summer evenings.
And when I was with her
I thought of it as
an occasion.

IN THIS ENDLESS WHITENESS

Mary Moore Easter

In this endless whiteness,
this five-month January of
multi-formed ice:
flat, opaque
solid and shiny
or
in particles so small and blown
they infuse the air, looking like
tangible fog
and quiet—

In this endless whiteness,
sea of faces pale,
drifted with pale hair
subdued, conserving—

Come three sisters,
Plumage shouting
Like tropical birds
Hair shorn
Bodies bursting.
Unexpected exotica
Transplanted from some technicolor
Zone.

No need to yell
"Give it out, sisters!"
They will anyway.

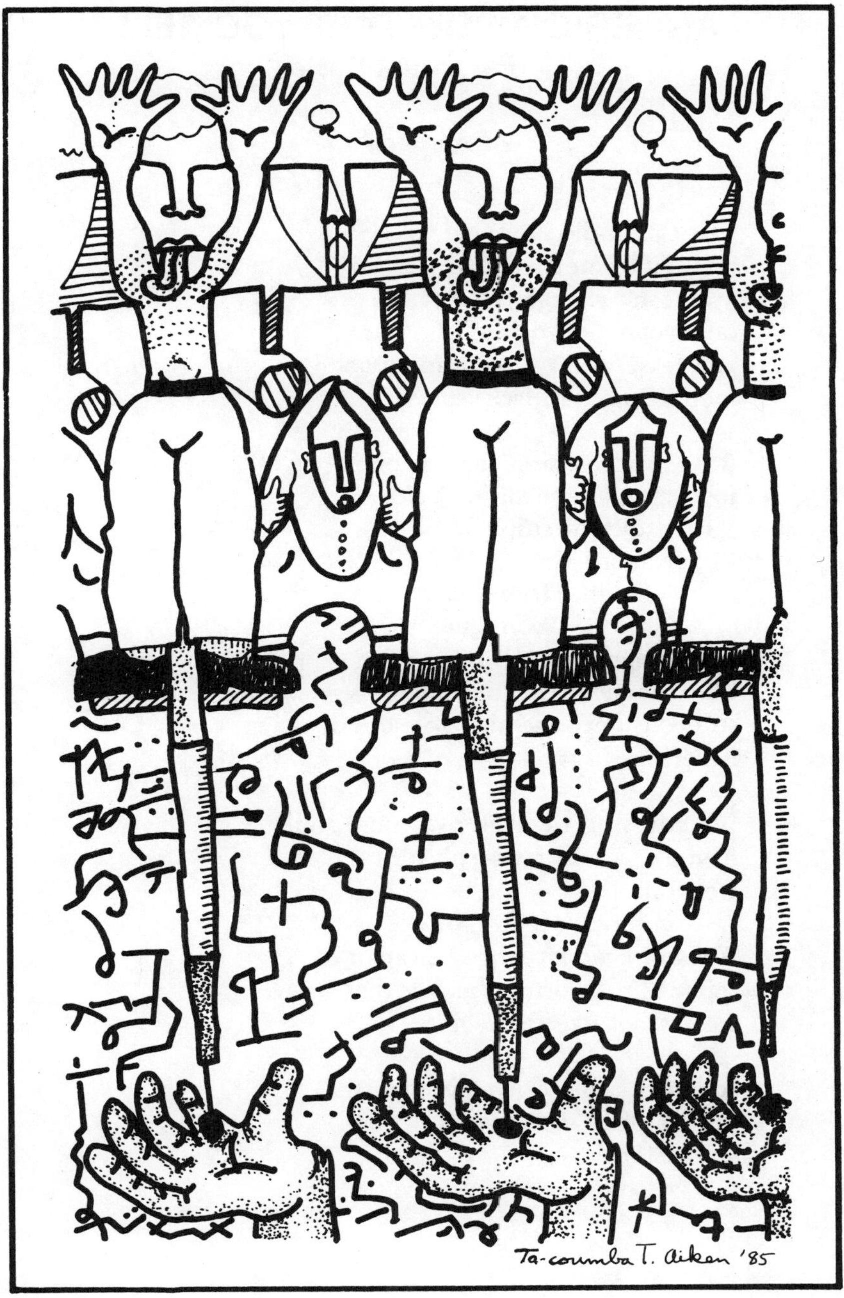
Ta-coumba T. Aiken '85

ANGER OR COULDN'T YOU TELL?
For Count Basie

Lynn McWatt

The Count died today,
and Catherine Deneuve says,
"you can't change the world,
only your moisturizer"
and Jesse won't stop running and
mobilizing the Black Vote ...

Reagan won't stop converting
foodstamps into military aid
for the dictatorships of
El Salvador,
       South Africa and
             Nicaragua
The hungry are still hungry ...
The homeless are still homeless ... while the W.A.S.P.
still consumes the biggest piece of the
American Crust ...

We still sing we shall overcome and
haven't ... which doesn't mean
we won't ...

We still keep chasing the carrot of
capitalism ignoring the fact that
we are not like the rabbit ...

Africa is still too irrelevant to the
masses of us, to learn its history ...
our history ...

and Sweet Count Basie plays
One O'clock Jump to the translated
rhythms of Africa's Julius Nyerere's
voice of WE
       MUST
           RUN
           while THEY WALK ...

and the Count died today ...

THE EMPRESS HAS NO CLOTHES

Lynn McWatt

Nudity proclaimed immoral when shown in Penthouse

(On a beauty queen w/ another women exempt from

public adoration.

       A change of heart by-passed a million copies sold
       Guccione, I'm S O r r y ! Invalid after 2 yrs.
       the perceived errors of youth are constant ...

Vanessa turns gray & passes torch of beauty & dignity to

a regretful but thankful Suzy.

       A triumph for morality ? or over-exposure ...
1st blk. & then blue/ Am. Greetings Hope
           for rain to cancel contract
             & nt. image.

P.S. Have you seen the pictures ?

OPINION

Lynn McWatt

Jesse/Womyn/V.P./Not of color

Feminizism/Diluted/from politics....

ALMOST AN UN-EXPOSÉ

Lynn McWatt

She burns/her halo of martyrdom
illuminates the porno rack/to a halt.

She rages/on nude/for strangers.

Who pay/Nothing/but attention.

BIG MAC ATTACK

Lynn McWatt

20 Dead
21 Affected
Killer is S.W.A.T.T.E.D.

dn.

Unanswerable questions
remain unresolved.

Once you fall off a horse
get back on ...

America's dream-scape
materialized into
an officer's date w/death
revisited ...

Sure, Hon, let's take the

kids to ...

INVOLUNTARY EMOTION

Jimmy Locust

My heartbeat changed in the middle of this song.
Perhaps it was a feeling I never wished gone.
But the feeling was alone.

Why would I call through the pain of the dying sun
and the cool brisk clear emotion, alone?

Is it something with a blink I faded out, or wished not
aroused?
But it was real.

All through dinner subconscious notions occurred and feeling
the music pull and play my hermit tone, — is that alone?

At one time I thought I bled it out through my emotional
movements on the floor before I teased my tongue with
bland broth with crisp corn nearly cooked, —
but it stayed it didn't leave me alone.

I glanced at the pain and the dying sun with cool brisk
clear emotion.

Then I was positive it was real.

I look at the black and white as I write and it turns
to grey, is it real or am I slipping away?

UNTITLED

Jimmy Locust

I sit and think of you as rumors of rain storm through
my past and this moment.

I see, feel and touch you as waxed ripples throw a
hologram in my mind.

I miss you.

I miss the wholesome, lonely emotionally-tied person
that in some odd way projects positive pure stimulation

I dont understand, spending 23 years beginning to understand
me, room for you is so vast but yet so narrow.

Selfishness within myself somewhat pushes you aside, which is
human, even in you.

That's why I don't flow through you as top of the hill
prairie wind cools my skin,
so by that trait we are alike.

When I think of you the sun and wind throws blue.
I miss you.

GRAVEYARD LOVE

George D. Clabon

I feel your absence
As I sit at the table
Sipping Sauvignon Blanc
Awaiting the dinner arrival
I feel the tug
From beyond the grave
At the root of my soul
And know how to escape not
For in my eye
I see the spectre of your smile
And hear your voice's laughter
At my comical remarks
While I'm alone

SOMEWHERE SOMEHOW

A. R. Simon

Somewhere, somehow
even before I reach adolescence,
the seed was planted.

> YE ARE THE FEMALE/DESCENDANT OF EVE
> ROOT OF EVIL/IN PAIN AND SUFFERING
> SHALL YE BEAR CHILDREN AND YE SHALL
> BE THE CARETAKER OF MAN.

Somewhere, somehow
while I played jacks, jumped rope
or watched Rocky & Bullwinkle,
somebody, somewhere, somehow
planted the seed.

> The message played over and over
> like the recorded voice of an
> answering machine.

Somewhere, somehow,
in between hopscotch, Tiny Tears, Barbie
and make believe toast,
somebody, somehow,
planted it.

> It had nothing to do with you.
> You and I were pawns in the great
> scheme of things.

Somehow, somewhere,
at age four, five or six,
or maybe earlier still
while I nursed at mother's breast
the seed was planted.

> Why else would a twelve year old's
> reaction to rape be guilt?

Somehow, somewhere
somebody, something
planted the seed in you.

> What had I done? Had I loved you
> too much Grandfather?

Oh yes, the ugly seed
had been planted
firmly,
somewhere, somehow.

> Did the sight of freshly washed and
> plaited hair excite you? Or were my
> shorts too tight?

Someway, somehow
you sensed it was there.

> It grew and blossomed into a
> THORN.

Oh God, somebody
somebody, somewhere
help me.

> You trembled as you pressed
> your body close to mine, whiskey
> breath pleading, pleading.

Somehow, someway
I've got to get away from him,
somehow.

> I trembled as the stubble from
> your beard scratched at my cheek.

But somehow
the THORN, the ugly
hideous seed, cut through my fear
like a sharp knife's edge
and somehow

> I shouldered the responsibility —
> for I knew/you knew, I could never
> tell.

They'd say "You provoked him
someway, You teased him somehow."

> They would've made your life miserable.
> My father would have killed you.

And so,
I kept silent somehow,
kept the ugly secret all these years,
somehow.

> You died and left me with it. I
> resent you for that.

And somehow I still feel
pity for you, somehow.
                    How is it that I can feel sorry
                    for you and shame for me?
Because somebody
somewhere, somehow,
planted the seed.

EPILOG

A. R. Simon

HAD A CONVERSATION TODAY
TALKED ABOUT RAPE
TALKED ABOUT THE WHY'S
THE WHEREFORE'S, HOW COME'S
WHAT IS, WHY IS THERE
                    RAPE

HAD A CONVERSATION TODAY
SHE NATIVE AMERICAN
ME AFRO-AMERICAN
BUT IT REALLY DIDN'T MATTER
COULD'VE BEEN
TWO INDIANS — TWO BLACKS
ASIAN-AFRICAN — JEWISH-POLISH
IT WAS STILL
                    RAPE

YES I HAD THE SAME
EXPERIENCE SHE SAID
LET'S TALK ABOUT IT I SAID
WALKING HOME FROM SCHOOL
HE FORCED HIS DOG ON ME
FORCED ME TO GO WITH HIM
FORCE ME TO SUBMIT FORCED
HIMSELF AGAINST MY
                    VIRGINITY

WELL I COULD NEVER TELL I SAID
WELL I DID SHE SAID
OH GOD I WISH I HADN'T
I CALLED THE POLICE
WENT DOWNTOWN YOU KNOW
HOW IT GOES THEY WANTED
EVERY LOUSY STINKIN
                    DETAIL

AND OF COURSE YOU WERE TO BLAME I SAID
OF COURSE I WAS SHE SAID
THAT'S WHY I NEVER TOLD
NEVER EVEN TALKED ABOUT IT
TILL A FEW YEARS AGO TOO ASHAMED
TOO SCARED 17 YEARS
                    AFTER THE FACT

YOU SHOULD WRITE MORE ABOUT IT SHE SAID
I DON'T KNOW IF I CAN I SAID
WELL YOU NEED TO GET IT OUT
TELL SOMEONE HAVEN'T YOU EVER
TOLD YOUR FATHER?

WHAT GOOD WOULD IT DO I SAID
IT WAS STILL
            RAPE

Don't Let Go Mommy!!!   Ta-coumba T. Aiken '85

FALLO MARSHES & BLISTER
COME TO MINNESOTA
(Part of a novel)

Alexs D. Pate

The dust rose across the horizon like billowing clouds of gnats toward carrion flesh. The sun, a bit player in the day's drama, set in a dim flicker of light. The scene, delicately eerie, had become Fallo's trademark. It seemed more often than not, his arrival into a city was accompanied by unpredicted weather and atmospheric giddiness.

Perched upon a slow moving horse, poised in thought, was Fallo Marshes, the famous singing cowboy from New Jersey. He had been in the saddle for more than fifteen weeks. He was thinking about a nice warm bed.

He was thinking about a nice warm bed in a simple, but sturdy wooden framed house, as a raging fireplace kept the walls dancing. He was also thinking that it would be complete if there was a woman, a soft, sensitive woman tending to his needs. He smiled. He thought of himself as drunk, comfortable, amorous. He sought relief through his fantasy.

Blister, unaffected by Fallo's imagination, clomped along. Being a horse, Blister cared less about fireplaces and such and was concerned with more immediate issues like what direction they were going and why. In the early evening light, Blister looked regal in his palomino color. The horse took great pride in his lineage and was quick to point out to Fallo that his ancestors would not have been caught dead under a singing Negro cowboy.

Yet, Blister did not regret his position. It was far better than what could have been, though clearly not as manficent as it might yet be. Blister considered himself an unabashed optimist.

Fallo had fallen on hard times. This was particularly ironic to Blister, for as his owner's fortunes diminished, so did his weight. This, of course, eased Blister's burden and made it difficult for the horse to be completely supportive of Fallo's quest for success.

Anyway, Blister figured that his handsome mane and his proud statuesque body would eventually be discovered and amply rewarded for his perserverance.

He hoped for television. Perhaps a series. Blister recognized that he would probably have to start at the bottom. But he had already resigned himself to accepting almost any type of show business work. He would even do commercials if it came to that. It couldn't be that bad, he reasoned, look at what Morris the Cat had accomplished.

Blister was prepared, even for the minor leagues. God forbid, but maybe he'd have to spend a year or two in the circus. How bad could it be? He realized the risks. It was widely known among horses that neither man nor beast escaped the circus environment unchanged. They said that the circus worked on you. A few months of the big top and bright lights could turn a horse against the silver screen.

So how bad was it to latch on to this fading star? Sure he was having a tough time. But with a little luck and the right timing, Fallo Marshes would be right back on top. And right under him, with equal billing, would be Blister:

FALLO MARSHES AND HIS FAMOUS HORSE BLISTER

It was fully night now. Fallo thought about his horse. Blister had been on his hooves for a long time. Maybe he should pull up at a 7-11 or a Roy Rodgers and get the old horse something to eat, he thought.

"I could use a cup of coffee myself," Fallo said aloud as he gently slid, ever so slightly, from side to side, as Blister carried him. "Say Blister, how about a little whoa at the next 7-11? That's a good boy." Fallo slapped Blister's neck with a force that would have sent a man reeling. Blister merely reared his head back in agreement.

They had been riding from Texas. Stopping here and there, Fallo would stake a claim on a busy street corner and croon his music to passersby. And those who stopped, staring, dumb-founded and speechless, would be treated to a truly different form of entertainment. With Blister not far away, Fallo would be standing there, creating an image that froze those who walked by. Fallo wore light blue calvary britches, with a gold stripe running down the side of each pant leg. His black, silk, double-breasted shirt would be open to the middle of his chest with a blinding yellow handkerchief tied around the inside of his collar with its ends resting gently on his brown chest.

His boots were of lizard and although they were encrusted with a thick coating of dirt, their quality was evident. The toe was pointed just enough to irritate easterners. His hat, the *piece de resistance* in the cowboy business, was a narrow, heavily rolled hat that curved down over his eyes and down the back of his neck. A feather snatched from the tail feathers of a squealing quail was pinned on the left side of the hat.

Fallo was a handsome man. His face was decorated with a thin, modest smile most of the time. His teeth were perfect. His smooth mahogany complexion seemed the ideal background for his warmth. Everything appeared correct.

He resembled Charley Pride, the country singer, although he was not nearly as heavy. Success was not draped about him as thickly.

Charley Pride angered Fallo. To Fallo, Charley had sang scads of borderline, red-neck songs for decades. This infuriated Fallo. Fallo had specialized in songs more of the western genre. He sang songs that made reference to tumbling weeds and prairie dogs. Songs about how whites had mercilessly destroyed a race of people in its quest for land and money. Songs about rattlesnakes.

When he would see Charley on television, perhaps on Hee-Haw, he would throw up. Among all of his habits, this was the one Blister hated most. It was Blister's major complaint of Fallo. Whenever he was completely revolted by something, he, without much warning would vomit uncontrollably. It is easy to understand why this upset Blister, as much as it was he who was beneath Fallo most of the time when the malady occurred.

Fallo would admit, albeit hesitantly, that although Charley Pride's selection of music was repulsive, he was proud to know him and considered it a feat for Charley to have become one of the nation's premier country singers. For a black man, Fallo reasoned, this was in the same category as running and completing the New York Marathon.

At forty-five, Fallo's face did not show marked signs of age. He was often pursued by women who might stop to hear him sing, but for some reason, women never figured much into his life. His music, his horse, his travelling way of life. They were important.

His audience, when he sang western songs, were much like Charley's: white, beer drinking cowboys and their women folk. But now, that had all changed. Now he was into a completely new thing.

It came as a shock of incalculable dimension to those in the show business world in Nashville and Memphis when Fallo announced to his peers and then to the world that he was leaving the Country and Western Club to play a different, perhaps more meaningful type of music.

The next morning, one of the local newspapers put it this way:

FALLO MARSHES TO PLAY REGGAE

Another led off its weekend entertainment section with the headline:

FALLO'S HAD IT WITH COUNTRY MUSIC
TO TRAVEL COUNTRYSIDE PLAYING REGGAE

and managed to misspell the name of his new music.

Of course, there was uproarious laughter heard all around him. Blister was completely confused. Fallo had not spoken with him about it. It was a stunned horse that bowed out of his last performance as the annual Nashville rodeo.

By the time they arrived back at the hotel, there were telegrams pouring in from all across the country. People wanted to know what was wrong with *their* music? Wasn't it the original American music? Was he turning out to be a communist after all? Hadn't they trusted him? Afterall he was a black shitkicker. Hadn't they bought his records? People were outraged. Most of those writing also asked one final question, "What the hell is reggae music?"

He received letters and telegrams from all of his admiring peers. Gladys Knight and the Pips wrote a long letter congratulating him on his decision, saying,

> *"... after so many ... so many ... years of barely knowing you existed (shoop shoop) we can now get to know ... get to know*

*... get to know .. get to know you and your (shoop shoop
shoop) music ... sweet music .."*

Richard Pryor wrote "I celebrate the founding of a truly New Negro Type, a Reefer Totin' Colored Cowboy." Peter Tosh, an important figure in the reggae music business accepted him cautiously, writing:

> *them that embrace the mystical and elevated rhythms of
> the sacred music for reasons other than pure love for Jah
> become the pawns of the drunken, power hungry bald-
> heads of Babylon. But if I and I are serious about the
> spiritual high of reggae music and endeavor to pursue
> the love of Jah and seek our movement from the madness
> of our oppressors, praise Jah. Jah righteous!*

Fallo noticed after a time that he had not received mail from either Charley Pride or Diana Ross. He wondered what was up with Diana? Was she too big to say what she thought? She could have at least wished him luck?

Maybe Diana knew exactly how the business world would react. Within fifteen minutes after his announcement he received a phone call from his agent, informing him that he no longer had a guaranteed source of income. His agent, Sylvia Butterman was outraged. It was her livelihood he was messing with. If she had anything to say about it, she said, he would never work legitimately again.

Privately he admitted to Blister that he hadn't expected such strong rejection from his previous followers and such derision from people he had expected to welcome him to a new way of feeling, of communicating. He had spent many evenings listening to Bob Marley, Black Uhuru, Jimmy Cliff, Yellowman and Big Youth in preparation for his transition. He had practiced and developed a new routine.

Included in his new act were a few original songs and some "covers" of existing music, principally by Marley and Cliff. He carried, as always, his guitar. But now he also carred a small snare drum and stand. He had learned to play that too while listening to the intoxicating reggae rythms.

Blister had tried to throw off the embarassment. At first it had been quite difficult. The horse was completely distraught. He could barely stand still while his owner perched himself on a milk crate in the doorway of an abandoned storefront and began singing such unusual music. But, more than being upset with the drop in status, Blister felt he had no role in his partner's newest endeavor. With western music he could occassionally join the entertainment by hopping on his two front hooves, bouncing like Trigger once did for Roy. But to this reggae thing, horses had no routine, no clue as to how to accompany even the nicest owner.

So he stood there, usually with his head turned in the opposite direction, flapping at flies with his tail as Fallo took up the Iri ritual.

2.

As Fallo and Blister turned onto Interstate 35W, heading into the City of Minneapolis, they faced an overcast chilly fall evening. They talked of the future. Fallo was saying to Blister that the trip to Minneapolis was significant. He was convinced it would bring them legitimacy. A change in their luck. It was a subject often discussed between the man and the horse.

"I can understand how you feel. I'm not blind Blister. Those folks ain't always happy to have me around."

Blister slowed his pace. He tossed his head back, irritated at his thoughts, "Really Fallo, what are you trying to prove? I'm just your horse, that's true. But I think I should have something to say about what's going on. For God's sake, man, it's my life too. Jesus. Why are you going to Minneapolis?"

Blister snorted and lurched forward a little faster. He was definitely irritated now. He was like that. He inherited it along with his sturdy back from his mother. He did not give Fallo a chance to digest the last question before he, without turning his head back, said, "No. Let me see if I can answer that. After having a quite successful career in Country and Western music, you decide that that's not good enough for you. You've got this message to communicate. Some deep social purpose is at the heart of it I suppose."

Blister's thoughts rolled out of his mouth and were immediately transformed to streams of light grey smoke which trailed behind him, flowing directly into the face of the receptive Fallo. The passing scenery disappeared and Fallo now saw only what Blister was saying. He could see the words take form within his mind. They were white on a dark background. He understood them.

As they rode, and as Blister talked, Fallo did not concentrate on anything but what Blister said. They had been through much together.

"So," continued Blister, "to the chagrin of nearly everybody who really cares about you, we go tromping, literally tromping off to San Antonio to take up on street corners singing reggae music. My word! Did you hear what I said? Do you understand what we are doing? Fallo, you are a forty-five year old black man who dresses up like a double positive of Robert Redford in the Electric Horseman. Talk about absurd."

"There there Blister. Thing's gonna be just fine. I know it's a little strange, me taking up reggae music like this." Fallo sat back in the saddle. He tipped his hat up a bit, he had a chin of grey and black stubble which his left hand was now pinching together as he talked.

"Have you listened to what I'm singing Blister? It's just different from any other kind of music I ever touched. It don't feel the same. It don't sound the same. Why . . . some people can't even dance to it. The rhythm is there. the beat is there, just like any other music. But when you go to put your foot down, something about it changes. And if you ain't careful, wham!, there you go . . . off rhythm." Fallo chuckled to himself as he visualized groups of people dancing to reggae music. A sea of people searching for the beat. An outpouring of affection for the music and a confused paralysis when they tried to figure out what to do with it.

"It's a freeing music Blister. If you could really understand what I'm talking about. I mean, if you could feel the freedom in that music. It's a protest music, I'll grant you that. The words are dire and demanding, but the music itself is giddy, it changes form, it's like clay. I have never experienced anything like it before. This is what music is supposed to be."

Blister was unconvinced. "Right now I'm more concerned about our reputations. After fifteen years of singing at hoe downs and appearing in rodeos all over the country, you are giving it all up to sing this crazy music for pennies. Where's that going to get you? Where's it going to get me? I have a life to be considered in this saga too you know. I don't want to be stuck up under you for the rest of my life. Give a horse a break, for Christ's sake."

No sooner had Blister punctuated his statement with a snort when they were startled by a splash of a puddle crushed by a speeding car. Blister was momentarily blinded. Fallo felt the water seeping through his pant leg and realized he had been sprayed as well. He shouted at the driver, who was now a diminishing smudge on the horizon.

"Goddamn cars. Goddamn drivers. You ain't the only ones on the road, you asshole."

Blister was recomposed and back in charge now. Fallo was hanging from Blister's side, holding on to the saddle and trying to wipe the mud from his pants. They were both silent. It was a ritual. While the car had not hurt them, it had served to announce their entry into the city. Minneapolis would be no different than the others, dominated by machines and unaccustomed to folks like Fallo and definitely not ready for a horse like Blister.

3.

"Where, may I ask, are we going?"

"Don't you know? I thought all you horses communicate with one another." Fallo spoke as he steered Blistro around a pothole in the shoulder of the highway.

"What are you talking about?" Blister coughed as he felt the reins pull sharply to the right.

"This is September right?" Fallo said into the wind.

Blister was becoming annoyed. "So it's September, so what."

"Blister, my faithful friend, I'm surprised at you. This is September and we're in Minnesota."

Blister heard the words, but was distracted for just a moment as a bus passed too close for his own sense of comfort. Fallo was essentially oblivious to such things as passing traffic aside for his occasional verbal barrages against cars. But it made Blister nervous to travel such busy highways.

He knew that once this road had been the world of his ancestors. A time when horses were exalted beyond all other forms of transportation. But things had changed. Somewhere in his deepest mind he was aware of his past and how significant he and his comrades had been. Now, as a species, they were remanded to service and entertainment. It was a dismal life where aspiration was choked off at early ages.

Blister turned his head back to Fallo and said, "We're assholes Master Marshes." Deference to Fallo's position as his master and rider was important at times. Especially when Blister could use it to his advantage.

The motor vehicles moved swiftly by. Untethered as they were, they crashed against the air with unmerciful force which made them not of this world to Blister. he could not imagine moving so fast. So fast that those whom one might pass would have no chance to contemplate your beauty or grace of style or anything. Just a cloud of grey black smoke and a flash of light. It was sickening, Blister thought.

Fallo, of course, was much less impressed by the fast moving metal vehicles. To Fallo they were merely a part of a nondescript landscape. Background noise to life. For Fallo there were only a few things comprising reality. His voice. His horse and the world his music created.

Having moved so abruptly from country and western to reggae had been easier for him than people thought. He had walked the higher ground of lyrics anyway. He felt a spiritual destiny in his heart. He lived the lives of thousands. He danced with no one for the sake of dancing. That reggae music should pull him was only natural.

They traveled the highway's shoulder in a momentary silence. Fallo thought about Blister's last condemnation. "We're assholes, Master Marshes." Fallo adjusted his body in the saddle. Blister's supple back was beginning to feel quite hard. They had to find some place to rest soon. As they approached the city, the lights began to glow on the new night.

Fallo's attention turned to the occasional discarded roadside litter. Fallo knew a lot about roadside litter. It was his hobby. Every now and then he would pull Blister to a stop, slide off the saddle and pick up some interesting piece of trash. Hanging from his saddle bag was another bag, a blue denim duffle into which he would stuff whatever things of interest he found. His hobby was not the collection of these items for the sake of collecting. In his spare time, when he was not on the road performing, he would create little sculptures of discarded, useless things. Much like those who worked with seashells, Fallo took great pride in his little creations.

But tonight he saw nothing which caused him to stop. Instead he found himself thinking about the Minnesota State Fair. It would be his first major challenge.

"Not going to respond master?" Blister would not be ignored. Even in the silence his anger grew. It was chilly here. Soon it would be downright cold. Why were they in Minnesota?

"Hmmm?" Fallo had lost the thread of their conversation.

"What in the name of Christ are we doing here? It's going to be winter soon. If we had any sense at all, we'd be heading south."

"It's very simple Blister. The State Fair. We're going to perform at the State Fair."

"Fallo, tell me the truth. Have you freaked out or what? What's a colored cowboy who sings reggae music going to do at the Minnesota State Fair?" Fallo flinched at the horse's tone and pulled the reins sharply, leading Blister off the freeway and into the city.

Blister continued, "Now I've heard everything. I thought you had some great master plan. But no. What the hell are you doing? Why are you taking me to some redneck state fair. This is more than even a faithful horse can take."

"You just don't understand Blister. I'm doing this because somebody has to. These people needs some education. They're too damn isolated up here from the rest of the world. I chose the Minnesota State Fair because it offers a large audience to share my music with. I'm finished with street corners and back alleys."

Blister listened and, as usual when he was perturbed, he broke into a trot, galloping harder, jostling Fallo roughly. He flung his head back, "Well, here to the end of street corners, but a state fair? Do we have billing?"

"Ummm ... will, I figured ..." Fallo stared off into space as he spoke.

"You figured what? You figured that we'd just come bopping into town, pull up at the local state fair and become a big hit. I swear Fallo, I can't believe you. You've really flipped this time. I'm just as crazy because here I am, carrying you into this godforsaken place. What do you think they're saying about us in Memphis?"

"I don't care Blister. Now's the time to get right with the music. To expand the universe through the rhythms of reggae music." Fallo, turned Blister down a large street.

People stared at them as they passed. It was a common experience for the horse and rider.

"So how are you going to play the state fair?" Blister was like a fired bullet. He never lost his place in a conversation no matter how many ways Fallo tried to divert him.

Fallo straightened his kerchief, pulled his hat further down on his head, "I'm going to camp outside the fairgrounds and play to the folks as they go in."

Blister picked up his pace. "Well, I don't want to go there. I have relations in that operation and I don't want to be embarassed. What will the other horses think if they see me standing beside some crazy colored cowboy?" Blister was really moving now and Fallo began to pull back on the reins in an attempt to control him. "Anyway, these folks don't know reggae music from a Hopi rain dance. I dare say, not many people do."

"That's all right Blister. That' why I'm going there. Protest is the spirit of life and reggae music is the purest of all protests." With that, Fallo broke into a song. Clomping along Franklin Avenue, feeling the warm rhythms, Fallo rared back and strummed on his guitar. Blistro's hooves hitting the pavement played off the drum beat.

Jah music movin
movin through the air
seekin the oppressor
seekin without fear
livin it
livin it

Bringing Jah music
To Babylon by horse
givin it to the people
throwin off the curse
livin it
livin it

Jah music movin
moving through the air
seekin the oppressor
seekin without fear
livin it
livin it

Fallo's head bobbed mightily as Blister gained even more speed. the words to the song were now barely audible to the people they passed. This suited Blister just fine. He hated the music. He thought about Hank Williams and Merle Haggard. What would they think? What would the folks at the fair say? "Oh my God Fallo, please stop. This is not going to work out at all."

"You say something, Blister?" Fallo was nearly out of breath from the singing and the early evening wind which weaved its way into his lungs as he expanded them.

Suddenly Blister began to slow down. "I think that perhaps we should stay here for the night, Fallo." Blister turned, without the guidance of Fallo, into the driveway of the Four Oaks Motel. "You've got money I hope."

"I told you in Des Moines I had money. Still got my savings. I don't know how long it's gonna hold out. Three thousand dollars don't last forever these days."

"You're telling me." Blister said, "Oats have gone sky high in the last four or five years. It's incredible. I just hope you've thought out a way to keep feeding me. Actually you've got to do more than that. In this place you had better find me a nice place to stay. I'm not standing out here all night in sub-zero weather. You can get that through your thick head right now, Master Fallo."

"I heard you pardner." Fallo muttered as he dismounted. Hitting the ground brought a strange sensation. He felt like he was full of little beads that were now being resettled throughout his body. He brushed himself off, tied Blister to a post which held up the canopy outside the lobby, and entered the motel.

The lobby area was small. A soiled burnt orange rug felt just a touch sticky under his narrow boots. Adjacent to the lobby was a restaurant where clusters of old people sat eating. Behind the reception desk was a young man. He stared at Fallo.

"You got any vacancies?" Fallo said, still looking in the direction of the restaurant.

"Yea, we got a couple. Forty-five bucks, ten dollar key deposit."

"Key deposit?"

"It's our policy to take a deposit on the key. Lot's of people leave out of here in the middle of the night. We have to change locks nearly every day if we don't charge. Don't make any difference though, they still don't leave the keys."

Fallo looked at the man. He didn't care about the details. He just wanted a clean room. The man seemed estranged from reality. He talked in a monotone drone which irritated Fallo.

"I'll take one." Fallo said to shut the man up.

"You want a single don't cha? I don't see nobody waiting," the man looked out the window, obviously looking for a car. It was then he saw Blister. "Oh my God. That's not .... Is that your ... that's a horse out there."

"You can't leave him there." The man backed away from the desk. He wasn't sure what was going on.

"Didn't intend to mister. That there is my horse. And my horse goes with me, so I need a ground floor room."

"You rode him in here? On his back?"

Fallo looked at the man, "You ever tried to ride a horse on his stomach?"

The man straightened his glasses which has slipped further down his nose. He then stood still, staring at Fallo. After a pause he said, "You with a rodeo or something?"

"I'm a performer and that there is my wonder horse, Blister."

"Well I don't know ... I ain't never allowed a horse to stay here before." The man fidgeted.

"You let the cars stay out there."

"Yes but cars are different ... this ... this is a Motel. It is for cars."

"My horse doesn't understand that. To him it's a comfortable place to spend the night. Got to keep him off the streets, you know. Now you gonna give me that room or what?"

"Just one night. Okay?" The man tried to smile.

"I like it pardner. I like it real fine."

Fallo paid the fee and returned to Blister. "Hey there horse, how're you doin'?"

"You don't care. You go in there, stay for God knows how long. Just leave me standing here, not knowing what the hell is going on. I don't appreciate it

Fallo. Are you going to stay here?"

"Room 343."

"Good then let's get on over there and I can relax. My nerves are shot to hell. By the way, I know you didn't ask him about anything for me to eat and I know you don't carry feed with you like you used to so, will you please order a bunch of hamburgers or something. I'm starving to death."

"Goddamn you Blister. All you do is complain. For a goddamned horse, you're an awful lot of trouble."

"Fallo Marshes, I resent that. I've done nothing but sacrifice for you." Blister stopped still as Fallo, holding his bridle attempted to continue forward.

Realizing that the horse had stopped, Fallo jerked his arm pulling the horses head forward. "Come on now Blister, I'm tired, please cooperate. Now git on!"

Blister would not move. Fallo pulled again. This time much more violently.

"So it's horse brutality now is it. You've stooped to new lows Fallo."

"Please Blister, let's just forget it tonight. We're both tired."

The horse pounded his front right hoof into the dirt and snorted, "I've had it Fallo. I can't take it anymore." With that Fallo threw his hands into the air, letting the reins go.

"When you get over this little fit of yours I'll be in my room over yonder. Let me get my saddle bag and guitar." Fallo removed the gear from the horse and disappeared into this room.

Blister looked around him. A new city, a new way of life. He had an urge to take off. Head south. But where would he go without Fallo? How could he go without Fallo? He was in the middle of nowhere.

The horse walked around the side of the motel and found a space where there were no cars where he could try to rest. His mind was very active though and he found it very difficult to relax. "I must get some rest. There's no telling what that man has planned for me tomorrow." He thought as he drifted into a vision of green pastures and rolling hills.

FAREWELL TO THE HIGHLAND LIGHT

Conrad Balfour

Dedicated to the three Gentlemen and a Whale: Bartleby, Captain Delano, Benito Cereno, and the Great White.

I'm an elderly man, one who senses what needs to be done in a world of peril. Given my occupation the ability to carry this off is almost conspiritorial.

I speak of the inspector—that solitary figure who bears pen and pad and is unfairly described as forcing and entering those pleasant establishments where the wearied traveler finds little appeal to vacate if the standards of sanitation are suspect. My description here is not to gain sympathy but to describe a most indifferent inspector, Irving White Coyote. He was more often called Benito due to a stint in the merchant marines where he sailed between Italy and New York harbor. His heritage was said to be a Negro father and a Passamquoddy mother, such union endowing him with qualities unfamiliar and foreign to one of my nature.

Never have I known one individual, except he be my God-fearing father, to impose such power or inflict such restraint upon my natural instincts as did Benito. Even to this moment my evaluation of the about to be told account leaves me confused, astounded, and with long periods of what I generously ascribe to myself as temporary inanition.

My name is Amasa Delano, and the year is 1949, a year when the sturdy seafaring town of New Bedford in my native state of Massachusetts, has call to summon up as much fortitude as once it did during a hundred years hitherto when a nation depended upon the whaler for lamp oil, lubricants, umbrellas, corset stays and cosmetics. In my youth I was plucky and often in opposition to tradition, but when I was admitted to the bar of the commonwealth, my zest for reform was substantial. Nevertheless my sense of fair play was not lost in the process of education. Because of this I was in opportune position to accept my present employment as contractor of Restaurant Inspections for Sanitation and Health for the state of Massachusetts.

My office rewarded satisfactory allowance, a staff of adequate personnel and a suite of conservative quarters where we were the single occupants. My east window would ordinarily look over the Atlantic if it were not for a swatch of an edifice directly to the starboard of us, a twit of a thing, barely an excuse for housing whatever mischief within its bleached planks.

My staff, civil servants, two gentlemen from Concord and Lexington, and a middle-aged lady by way of Andover, satisfied the many demands of the dining stops that dotted the rugged landscape like buoys plopped into the sea from Plum Island to Montauk Point.

Kurdish was the senior staff member, medium stature, built like a spool of telegraph wire, cheeks inscrutable, a mustache blacker than the pit of Hell, and an assortment of neckerchiefs and turtleneck undershirts to outdo the stock of Pittman's haberdashery. Kurdish usually wore an outer shirt with its sleeves rolled above the elbows giving him the appearance of a stevedore from the Hinghan yards. He also sported a bowler that drew cast-down-eye-attention in this New England town.

Second in seniority was CM, those Roman letters signifying the numerals 900, and which Kurdish and Missy, she being my female employee, claimed in humor that the bearer of those letters was older than Solomon. And indeed CM was a first hand witness to blizzard, hurricane, drought, prohibition and the stock market crash plus other historical blights that pocked yankee history. CM was an incessant tea drinker, crackling the bag of Salada on an early Monday, dipping the packet for a precise twelve seconds before extracting it like a Block Island salt pulling up line, then depositing the teabag in an extra cup for the forthcoming Tuesday, except this time the allotted submergence was expanded by two additional seconds, and so forth through the working week until on Friday the milkless tea was devoid of even a scintilla of spice.

Missy reminded me of a poisonous plant: Belladonna or Mandrake, her vertebrate bumping along under her skin in the most peculiar places, opening her up where she should want to be closed and vice versa so that as she approached one the feeling was an ominous sensation of impending envelopment. God help the superstitious proprietor of establishments inspected by Missy in such reverent towns as Tiverton, Seekonk, or North Carver, who I suspect would rather exceed the codes levied upon their kitchens than face up to a return examination by my employee.

Industrious as my staff was, there was a need for greater work in the immediate future, for as I previously stated, eating establishments were rapidly multiplying, government conscription providing sailors the opportunity to savor the delicacies of mackeral and lobster.

In answer to my advertisement—but allow me to be more precise; Kurdish, following his unanswered rap upon my door, entered my office and announced that a strange man was now ascending our stairs, he, Kurdish, affording a premature view of the visitor by vantage of the jutty-window in his quarters that formed a hypotenuse from the upper floor to the lower front door.

"Mr. Delano, whatever else it is not, it IS an oddity."

"Mr. Kurdish, you mean he—he—is an oddity." I was not without erudition for one never knows what linguistic encounters an inspector may experience in the service of the commonwealth.

Kurdish pressed on with infinite trivia; "Whatever sir, but to say—he— may be stretching it a bit."

With a nervous cough I suggested that Kurdish show the visitor into my office when he arrived.

"Are you sure sir?"

I assured him that I had no reason to speak idly accenting my intentions with a dismissing lowering of my chin into a sheath of application forms at which time Kurdish shuffled away.

The morning was one peculiar to the coast—grey seas with a sheet of sky closing out the sun as an unpainted board slides across a dirty skylight. The sea was ethered as if the ashes of Hell had been sifted from its furthest extremities and shaken through a chimney upon grates of the New Bedford horizon. The labored gulls reflected no white this day, indeed the murky wings seemed to crack through the haze rather than flow, the effort jerking them into confusions rather than symmetry.

In the outer quarters there was a like absence of activity, and with patience straining as if some impure essences were screaming to break from beneath the sinews of my being, I scraped my Captain's chair across the floor, rose and walked from my office to investigate whatever fates lay behind the portal.

Fate indeed. I have seldom encountered such a radical connection to another human. Professor Coleridge hurling his pointer against the Atlas when an undergraduate challenged D.H. Lawrence's authority to speak for a woodsman when his own upbringing was hardly one of sexual gratuities (of course the undergraduate was entirely incorrect); the Coalition to Preserve the Existence of Invertebrate Animals picketing the law offices of Pickering, Pickering and Bryde, a 45 year old legal firm on Boston's Atlantic Avenue where I was an understudy during the year they defended Seafaring Union #153 the right to drag the harbor for razor clam, quahog, basket cockle and periwinkle; or on a more personal note that occasion on the Public Transportation System whereupon reading my Globe on a crowded bench, I was suddenly startled by a roughly clad body, its posterior poking onto my newspaper, then in short time the remainder of the torso collapsing helplessly into my lap, disturbing my Dodds and causing me no shortage of embarrassment. But these few categories weigh in no lesser or greater impact than that of my first laying eyes upon Mr. Irving White Coyote, more commonly known as Benito.

This creature of the earth was hefty of frame. His skull was tall. I say tall. I do not say round or square or stubby or scrimped. I could almost envision myself stripping away his skin from its skull and then having room enough to walk through its open jaws. I admit to an exaggeration when I say his temporal bones might have harbored 320 ounces of brain. Benito's body was so enormous and his features so babylike I could well imagine that he was growing eight weights to the hour, a suckling giant with the milk of life coursing through his organs and rapidly consuming every measure of lactate possible for its ravenous metabolism. His hair lay flat across his head like an owl's nest, the black strands gelatinous and awry, in need of brush despite the useless accessory. As if having no need for keen vision, Benito chose to adorn his pate with sunglasses. I could understand its purpose if it was to soften the sight of his view upon his belly which was of eminent girth. I fantasized it filled with rubber boots, tinfoil, wicker baskets and the spigot from an oxygen tank.

He wore crumpled white. Crumpled white blouse with ivory buttons, crumpled white trousers and a crumpled white tie on his invisible neck. Benito was an astound. A force. Lastly, he sported a black cane with an indifference of manner that it was patently insulting to think that any material aid could properly support such ponderous weight. Its grip looked to be of sturdy sapling that woodsmen find in the forests of Maine, inlaid with burnished brass handy enough to withstand a twin charge of powder, its shaft gnarled and highlighting nothing, so black and dark that it appeared an extension of Benito's hair, and as he leaned in precarious slope upon it, I anticipated that Benito had successfully harpooned the office floor and was not about to let it get away.

Nor I him. The excessive workload, the inconvenience of soliciting more interviews, compelled me to place the needs of the office ahead of petty impressions. My request to Kurdish that he introduce me to the gentleman met with silence. The silence is familiar; a glance, a further glance filled with hollow look suggesting snuffed candlelight which normally illuminates the passage of words, then of course one finding himself taking up the slack, leaping into the breach, bunging the cask. I would speak with Kurdish another time about this—his lack of deportment I took as a reflection upon my person.

"I am Amasa Delano. Please sir, won't you come into my office?"

I motioned him to me and upon seeing my gesture, a waffling shiver of frame veered imperceptibly toward me and was at my side as a giant ship that slips upon you like lightning within a glacier. I steered him into the friendlier harbor of my office.

Our words were few. My first impression heightened over this mixed barrel of blood. Stoicism was an inherent trait with our native Americans, a quality that my fellow attorneys could better practice, but I thought it inhibitive for the Benito's who were born with it. That combined with those good natured properties endowed in the Negro enhanced my judgment of this strange person now embracing my offices. Since Benito said little I was afforded the time to weigh my thoughts of his worth to the firm. How would he fare? Stoicism? That could very well be an advantage in those dining places filled with cheer and high living. Good nature? Remarks are more flippantly hurled from the intoxicant. A man with tender character is more likely to survive the spleen of boisterous seamen.

I summoned CM for a cup and packet of his tea. He popped his head into my quarters, heard my request, then with a nod pulled away as a rowboat from the mother ship.

I should have stated before that glass folding-doors divided my premises into two parts, one of which was occupied by my inspectors, the other by myself. According to my humor I threw open these doors, or closed them. I planned to assign Benito a corner on my side of them so as to have this quiet man within easy call.

At first, Benito's work was prodigious. Mornings were devoted to the inspection. Afternoons were given to the office where he filed reports of those establishments derelict in their obligations. By dawn Benito was up and away motoring in his rusty white Plymouth the sturdy hamlets of the land; Horseneck Beach. Nonquitt. Little Point. Fall River. South Swansea. Ocean Grove. Rehoboth. Dighton Rock. Massasoit. Scotland. Winneconnet. By twelve tolls of Trinity Church his vehicle sputtered before the east end of the building, stopped before a waste-bin that pleaded 'KEEP NEW BEDFORD TIDY' and out would emerge the breaching Benito with satchel and cane tucked into his voluminous armpits.

Of course the daily inspections, although lacking in that excitement given more to the crew of whalers, was by dint of its nature the fundamental framework of the entire profession. But I can hardly impress upon you that the unglamorous office work was more critical to the efficiency of this operation. Forms were filed in triplicate, typed neatly, judgments and collaborating statements put into print, citations administered, rationale for all actions verified, loopholes, legalities, interpretations, statutes, ordinances, settlements by verbal agreement. As with law enforcement agencies, discovery was important, but proper administration insured resolution of any offense. When those duties became taxing it was my fortunate resource to beckon my staff for a discussion. One objective I had in placing Benito so handy to me behind a screen, was to avail myself of his services on those occasions. Possibly ten days had passed when I summoned Benito to check over a recommendation for the State Inspection Board to temporarily suspend a dining establishment, which name is best left unrevealed here. Imagine my fluster when without moving a jot from the folding chair at his desk, Benito mumbled, "I would prefer not to."

This was improbable. Did my staff overhear this? Ah, vanity in the face of a quick turn of expectations. Maybe Benito heard me incorrectly? But his answer to my repeated request was duplicated. "I prefer not to."

"Prefer not to! What do you mean prefer not to?" I crossed the room rapidly, papers at fingertips, darted behind the screen and thrust the documents upon his desk where they kited to an upright landing. "Are you ill? There's work to be done here man!"

"I would prefer not to Massa."

"Massa?"

"I would prefer not to."

"Did you say Massa?" He was silent. "If you DID say Massa, then you go far astray. Now you know that my name is Amasa. I PREFER Mr. Delano." How easily my thoughts abandoned the primary issue here. Massa. Massa. How could he? How insidiously clever if Benito's intent was to guilt my conscience. How evilly clever if his design was to deflect me from that function which would have engaged him in what he might consider menial work. My name was never a problem. Never thrown into my face like an eastern gale. What right has he for even an innocent slip of the tongue? What right? I looked at him. Calmly. Thumbing through his reports unruffled as a weathervane. Seconds ago I could have dismissed him, but the passage of moment, the conflict of mind, the strangeness of this event, stayed my haste. As it was I would rather have thrown

164

into the street my India Rubber Plant than evict the odd, remarkable, eccentric Benito Irving White Coyote. Somehow I was capable of repossessing my documents, spend a last lingering stare at Benito's cetacean form, and then reseat myself at my desk. Thoughts played within my head but the dwindling hour induced me to summon Kurdish who took care of the matter.

Later, while coastal residents were recuperating from a stinging storm, I scheduled a staff meeting given the delay of production due to climactic conditions. I called Kurdish, CM and Missy from their adjoining office to join me and Benito at my desk. As they settled in I called to my newest employee.

"Benito! Why do you delay?"

I heard the creak of his folding chair violate the floorboards, and his weighty mass seemed to tilt the room as he stood by the screen.

"What do you wish?" was his question.

"The schedule, the schedule," I said impatiently. "We are prepared to discuss our schedule. Come"—and I motioned in much less a convivial manner than that which first beckoned him to my quarters on that first day.

"I would prefer not to," he said, and quietly evaporated behind his screen.

I was flabbergasted. Here was an act of piracy—almost. Here before my crew, my subordinates, my . . . I fortified myself with an extraordinary inhalation, advanced toward the screen, and adamantly demanded of Benito what he was about that required such unmeritorious conduct. "Why?"

"I would prefer not to."

It should have been the breaking of us, a stamping of differences labeled irreconciliable, an immediate discontinuity of any further relations. But there was something of Benito that held me in abeyance, even a gentle sort of warming toward him. A need to reach and understand.

"This is to your benefit that we acquaint ourselves with the new schedule. It will enhance your production. Won't you familiarize yourself with it? What is your reply? Benito!"

"I prefer not to," he repeated in a blowing-like manner. It was a most puzzling situation. At this moment I felt not the slightest iota of disrespect, and in retrospect I can honestly state there are various irreverences that emanate from a normal staff of employees, but administered in such subtle ways that the employers have to pass them off as the pains of leadership, but that nevertheless reveal more disrespect than that of my newest inspector.

"You have firmly made up your mind Benito to disregard a cooperation that would affirm greater knowledge of your future duties?"

He substantiated my observation with an assurance that my judgment was correct and that he had clearly stated his position. My only course toward dignity was to turn the matter over to the gaping eyes of my underlings for their opinion and remark.

"Kurdish, how does this affair strike you now?"

"It strikes me odd sir. I take my judgments from their sources, do I. I'd be a lookin' at that a bit more carefully sir."

"Missy, what is your opinion of this unusual behavior?"

"Well Amasa, we do have a queer one now. Not surprising however, if you know what I mean. These things do have precedents."

"Do you hear Benito? Do you?" I was speaking through the screen as if it were an extension of his incredibly small ears. "They all commiserate with me. Now come out here and see to your duty!"

But the silence resounded through the quarters. I probably pouted. I'm certain I flushed and furrowed my brow. But the pressures of time again overwhelmed the situation and business was conducted without our unusual apprentice. However this was not to say that business was exempt of grumbles and insinuating remarks directed toward our leviathan in the next partition.

Some days passed, my inspector conducted his morning visits according to his own whims, gave me no cause for alarm, but to the contrary, demonstrated a knack for calling on a territory that amazingly avoided any conflict of overlapping with the remainder of the crew. I observed him carefully. Promptly at noon he slid his great bulk into the office, moved behind the folding-screen and conducted his affairs. He never went to dinner. My staff engaged in supping prior to the afternoon stint in their office so as not to waste the hour. But Benito faithfully conveyed an oily white parcel containing an enormous sandwich, which once it was my fortune to observe, consisting of a loaf of grey biscuit-like bread that Benito artistically sliced with a sort of flensing tool as if it was blubber from a bowhead whale. Upon the bread he placed an interesting grey fishy substance, then compressing the entire conglomeration he laid the sandwich to rest across his flat tongue, chomped his dentures around the mass, and then with the oddest of squishes he worked the contents of his mouth into what I had to believe was a pulpy mash, before giving off an exhalation that seemed to strain the unwanted matter back into the oily paper.

There was no disturbing Benito during this ritual. It took one hour, one hour to the minute before he completed his daily repast and tended to his reports. It was as if he was submerged beneath the platform of time and could not be called to surface until his hour had transpired. I could hear him blowing from his cubicle as if to signal his re-entry into the world of humans.

Poor fellow I thought. It's no fault of his own. How peculiar he must feel with habits so unlike any of his peers, and how can one blame that sort if his wish is to isolate himself, prudent or not, from those of us with more normative habits. He means no harm to any soul. He's never been unproductive. Lord knows he has every right to turn down his tail and depart from these quarters for friendlier circumstances. I can get along with Benito. I will. If I turn him out no telling into whose hands he may fall. Certainly to a far less understanding agency than this. Yes, this was his home. And in this refuge I can extend all the hospitality sorely absent from a society oftentimes as cold as the Atlantic. Still, Benito had his way, one of irritance and mood. A way and a disposition that tested me to the fullest. New challenges reared gargolian heads. I had as much impression upon him as a kick to the kelp beds that dot the southern seas. Would it be that I was a grizzled captain on 'the other side of land' where my word was absolute law and my standing as high as God almighty. But not so. The occasion was thus:

"Benito, I notice that you call on but one establishment a day. Is there a reason for this reduction of work?"

"I prefer not to."

"What? Are you some sort of slogan? What is it you say? Do you mean that you prefer not to explain your daily charge?"

"I prefer not to Massa."

"Good heavens Benito, surely you don't mean to persist in this intolerable mispronounciation of my name? No more of that, do you hear? No more!"

I stormed from his cubicle and glaring at Kurdish and CM, angrily exclaimed, "Benito persists! He is derelict in his morning duties! What do you say about it Kurdish?"

Kurdish stroked his mustache and with exceptional intensity he barked, "What do I say sir? I say flay the monster! His skin would better serve as a tablecloth in the Gruel and Suds than taking up space here!" And with that colorful assail Kurdish rose to his sturdy legs and made for the cubicle. But I, not yet to that position, detained the angry Kurdish with a remainder of our inherent civility.

"Sit down Kurdish, now do my man, it will see us well to hear what CM has to offer."

"I'm shocked sir. But excusing me, I think I know the solution to the matter. Something to drink sir. Something strong I mean. None of this tea and milk, not for the likes of that hulk. And begging your forgiveness, if I may suggest it, a little closer lobtailing to the fairer gender, if'n you now what I mean."

I appreciated the candor of my veteran inspectors if not their wisdom. "Thank you. Thank you all. I shall take what you say under consideration," and with that charity returned to my office where again I felt attached to Benito by my very proximity to his cubicle. In addition an empty powerlessness came over me and in blind overture I gravitated to the screened-off area and confronted Benito once again.

"Benito, I do prefer you to make multiple calls each each day."

Heavens above, was that me speaking?—'I do prefer'—it's contagious! By the angels in Paradise it is contagious!

"I prefer not to."

His stereotyped response caught me unawares given the way my mind wandered. "What's that Benito?"

I flushed and spun dizzily to my desk, head in hands, the picture of dejection. Is there no answer to this human mystery? What is my sin? And if in its discovery, what do I offer in repentance? I called from my retreat. "Benito."

Silence from him.

"BENITO!"

Silence.

"BENIIIIIIIIITO!"

Like a 200 ton Blue he glided to the folding screen, maw agape, looming in a white colonnade of rumpled power, cane a mere twig in his fluke-like arm and fist, a hill of ivory, ancient, faintly yellowed, indomitable.

"Go there," I nodded to the door, "and fetch Missy."

"I prefer not to," and he swiveled on his support to disappear behind his blind.

"Certainly," I said in defeat, sighed myself away from my desk, and retreated from the disquietude of my office toward the sanctity of the salt outdoors. As I passsed through the outer area, I was faintly aware of the whispering amongst my staff, but I had little inclination or strength to give it any attention.

It was a fact. A queer employee with eccentric patterns was now in control of a professional attorney whose heart was bent on human understanding but only rewarded with heavy consternation. My staff was whispering, my staff was disjointed, my staff was adrift.

Days passed. I had much opportunity to think. No matter what, Benito was an honest man. He has never disturbed money or valuable papers that found their way to our coffers. Again, I repeat, I trust him. And, he is the first to leave in the morning—evidence of such due to Benito signing a gasoline voucher at my desk each day before he departs and prior to my arrival for work—and he is the last to leave at night. There are four keys to our suite of rooms. I have one, Kurdish and CM have theirs, and Benito the last. Missy chooses not to enter this solitary building alone, therefore has declined the privilege. Yes, I can trust Benito. I've noticed that he wears his key at the end of a leather cord that encircles his neck, or at least around the lower extremity of his head as I don't believe the man possesses a neck. Usually the key is hidden from view, but at times, depending upon the lean of his mass, the cord falls away from his blouse and the key is visible. Obstinancy on my part saw me continue to request certain duties of Benito, knowing full well that they would be rebuffed, the only concession being a reduction of demands. I could not get him to call on more than a single establishment per day. His daily routine was an early start, the singular call, his return at noon when he consumed his unpalatable sandwich, which I facetiously identified as a diet of krill, plankton and herring, and that for a precise sixty minutes, then complete his forms that for the life of me remained a puzzlement. Indeed, this was Benito's home, possibly his last safe refuge. I well imagined that he'd been in so many institutions of work and tormented by a society traditionally cruel and remonstrative to the likes of such as my inspectors, that the second floor offices in this coastal town building were a comfort to him. I was no less disturbed by his reserve, no less by his damning independence, no less by his stoicism. But for the most part I was resigned to all this. After all what would Benito do without me?

One Sunday morning I was early for services at our local Presbyterian chapel, and eagerly discovered myself needing to stroll around to the office. The air was clear with a snap to it that moistened the eyes and cleansed the soul. The sea was running. Along the broken sandline discarded surf gasped for life as white swabbings evaporated moments before new arrivals washed ashore to take their place in this moveable burying ground.

Turning the key in the street level door, I was overcome by a pervasive sense of my existing in some other dimension. I don't recall my feet touching the steps, but ascension was a reality for there I was, before the upstairs door, about to turn my key in the lock. From inside I heard the ethereal wail of—of—whatever, reverberating through the paneling in a quiet power that could well have emanated from the deepest pregnancy of the ocean. I stood transfixed as the echoes and melodious waves stirred faint breezes in my consciousness. I stood fully six minutes before the notes diminished, fading like retreating moonsilver as the clouds replace the evening illumination.

On opening the door my nose detected what I thought to be sperm oil. My head was swimming as I stepped gingerly toward the tall folding-screen where instinct told me I would find the object of this current mystery. Could I? Could I tread unannounced into the private sanctum of my strangest employee?

"Benito." It was tentative. "Benito, are you about?"

I moved to the junction of space where access afforded me instant understanding. Benito slept here. Why—he slept in these quarters. Oh, the poor man. I am sorry for him. How frugal of the poor soul. How thrifty. And how embarrassing for Benito to find that I've discovered him.

Upon his desk I saw a lamp, green shade, oil base, unlit now, but one of those treasures often sought by travelers to this land. Pressed into the folding-chair was Benito, the girth of him so large that the chair nearly surrendered itself to his bulk. Before him on the beaten desk was the carnage of his breakfast, what remnants remaining allowed me little opportunity to distinguish its identity. Astride his nose rode the dark glasses. Prior experience proved Benito's acoustic perception intensely keen. His vision was marred more by optic mirror than degenerate nerve, but perhaps this colossus had little need for visual perfection. At times I was of the view that he had a parasite in his ear, an infection of sorts. How else to explain his constant ignoring of my call until well into multiple repetitions? And then he tilted his head in that way as if to defend his healthy ear from my vexious beratings. But even with that, I was sure that his one good ear was enough to detect the slightest stirrings from the bowels of the sea.

Above his desk, pinned to the wall, in those multi-colors preferred by cartographers, hung a large map of the eastern seacoast. I was too distant to make out specific sites, but along the blue ocean were blue-headed pins, and upon the white land, white-headed pins. You must realize that I took all this into my view in a matter of moments, feeling like a skipper of a vessel boarding a foreign ship who upon pulling himself above the bulwark sees all the crew and interior spread before him for instant scrutiny.

"Benito, I'm sorry. This must be very difficult. I wasn't aware." With that I stepped into his territory, adjusted my eyes and peered curiously at the map. There were four blue pins in the northern latitude. The first was at Queen Elizabeth Islands with the red calligraphy; 100 latitude, 30 longitude. Then a pin at Devon Island; 95 latitude, 30 longitude. Barrow Straits; 95 latitude, 35 longitude.

And finally Lancaster Sound; 80 latitude, 35 longitude. Upon the land the white pins indicated; Fort Phoenix Beach, Fairhaven, Mattapoisett, East Marion, Acushnet, Wareham, Buzzard's Bay, Onset, and Monument Beach.

When I turned my head to seek explanation from Benito what this strange tracking was about, he anticipated my query with, "I prefer not to explain anything." I attempted to shift the subject matter and inquire of Benito's history, but he showed no interest.

"Fine Benito. Let's not ask any more of your background. But won't you do the work that I ask of you? See here my man. I want to help. Why won't you allow that?" Benito staunchly kept his distance and in return, shaking my head, hands clasped behind my back, I informed Benito that I was forced to consider whether giving him an extra month's wages and dismissing him was not the best solution for both of us. But even this evoked no stirring, so muttering something about tardiness for holy services, I turned on my heel and descended to the quiet street still shimmering in the sunlight.

But church was no longer in the picture. I wandered the New Bedford streets thinking of my threat to Benito, thinking of that peculiar map with its puzzling blue and white pins. I could not recall all the towns, but it seemed to me that they corresponded to Benito's daily inspections. I made up my mind to have another look at all this.

Monday morning, with Benito up the Cape, I entered his work area and stood looking at his desk with the now unadorned wall. No doubt the map was in his desk. Feeling no pangs of guilt, confident in the security of whose property this really was, I slid open the drawer and extricated the folded map. I opened it full upon Benito's desk, pressed my fingers over its surface feeling the disturbed punctures made by the pins now sittling idly in the ladle of the drawer. As I suspected, the route of Benito's daily calls methodically made their way up toward the arm of the Cape, while the perforations of blue pins in the northern latitude descended as falling stars, in my judgment approximately 75 miles per day. Where would Benito travel to this day? My interest was whetted. I anticipated his return, but no, I anticipated entering the office again the next morning as I was unwilling to reveal that I was spying on his uncommon chart.

At the moment there was no further thought of dismissing Benito. But some days transpired when a new crisis entered the picture. Benito refused to fill out his reports.

"But why Benito?"

"I prefer not to," came the unescapable cant.

I was as persistent, I implored until he stared at me with those dark eyes covered with his acre of brown lens, and whispered, "Don't you even know why?"

"I do not." I was stunned by this rare non-declarative expression. He refused to enlighten me and in the next few few days I attempted to conjecture what it was Benito was implying. As with everything else about him, this too came up with no resolution.

He returned later each day. Ate his lunch and as before stayed past the departure of the last staff member. It wasn't long before Kurdish requested an audience with me, and speaking for CM and Missy, declared that they were all fed up to the forecastle with the blatant delinquencies of Benito and they felt unrestrained in disregarding more than a fair share of the work.

"So, it's mutiny is it?" I thought it juvenile the moment I uttered those words.

"Fair practices sir. We share your sensitivity toward the hardship cases in our world, but we think in this instance it be ill-advised."

"I understand, Kurdish. Of course. Let me have time to think upon your words."

That day I gave Benito one day's notice to leave the premises, and offered the poor man a generous extra month's salary in order to salve his pride. "And Benito, please leave the key under the mat this evening. I expect you to spend this last week in more appropriate settings."

The next morning, to my disappointment, beneath the mat was a collection of dust, lint, tinfoil, a wooden matchhead, but alas, no key. Benito's personals were intact. I studied the chart again. The northern perforations descended to Prince Regent Inlet, 90 latitude, 40 longitude, and Baffin's Island, 80 latitude, 50 longitude. Likewise Benito's inspection trail traversed back and across, yet indomitably forward toward the tip of the Cape. I was struck by the strange route—Sagamore, Sandwich, Pocasset, Silver Beach, Falmouth, Woods Hole, Teaticket, Popponosset Beach.

That evening Benito arrived with hostile looks from his office peers, but seemingly disregarding these, he rolled into his cubicle and sat at his desk as firmly as an isotope imbedded in rock. I followed him to his area, noticing the cord around his neck, my dangling key sitting upon his chest, tarnished and as a talisman exerting a power over me that permitted only a watered-down demand on why he returned when I had ordered him out.

"I prefer not to."

"Will you or will you not depart these premises Benito?"

"I would prefer not to leave."

"Then for heaven's sake man, won't you do the work?"

"I prefer not to."

"Well then you must leave. I cannot take responsibility for you any longer. You've created an eruption amongst the staff. You have no right here. There's criticism from other quarters also. The banker. The retail store. Others. They've noticed your lack of cooperation. They choose to name it belligerence. You see? You must leave. I have no choice. Please understand. But whether you do or you don't, you must leave."

"I prefer not to."

"Good God Benito, who commands this ship? You? It certainly appears so! I depart for my apartments now! Be gone when I return!" And saying that I left the suite and headed for a tidy living room and a spot of tea.

Later that night, the moon falling full upon the red bricks and weathered planks of the New Bedford domiciles, I made my step to the office, and upon unlocking the upper door, discovered that Benito had not moved from the premises. I became angry. I raised my voice. I extended him every opportunity to respond. But no—all I gained was the guilt of an interrogator. He was in his private space. I decided to remain silent. Unbelievably I again felt sorry for Benito. I'd wait him out. The hour was late. Upon his wall hung the map, pins mounted. Can there be something to this map that can unravel all my pain? I'm discouraged with him. With my failures. With the staff. Even with my peers. What should I do? I'll be exhausted by morning. I can solicit a locksmith and change the key. But I cannot be cruel to Benito. No. I don't dare to remove his belongings. Look at him. A presence. A mammoth. Holding on where he's been repudiated. It's as if one day he believed he might become extinct, as if this clinging on, this barnacle-like behavior, adhering yet rejecting at the same instance, was a kind of protection of his personal species from the maladies of the white man. Well, I have no other option. He won't quit me. But I can quit him. The building across the way, sorry as it is, still has an unobstructed view of the sea. It has space. This I'm aware of. I can move our belongings there in short time.

The chart on the wall had its southernmost pin at Foxe Basin, 75 latitude, 55 longitude. Benito on land had waveringly advanced to Mashpee and Barnstable. I was tired. I had to come to a plan of action. I left the office and headed toward the comfort of my blanket and headboard.

The next afternoon I informed Benito that our offices were relocating across the street to the white building, and that he had best find himself different quarters. "Good bye Benito." He made no reply. Three days later we had moved, our new offices now adjacent to the International Whaling Commission.

A week went by. I received a visit from a man I recognized as the absentee landlord of our previous suite. "Sorry to disturb you sir. I seem to have an unusual problem. I believe he was your apprentice. An odd sort of gentleman. Still hanging out there. Discovered him when the painters arrived. Well, he won't move it seems. Asked him myself I have. Queer sort of reply—prefers not to. I wondered if you had any ideas on the subject? If not it will have to come to bodily ejection although I admit I don't look forward to tackling that type."

I made it clear that there was nothing I could do explaining as best I could some of the basic problems engendered by my former employee.

One week to the day this same landlord called on me once again. He was in an apoplexy, his forehead wrinkled and red and his cheeks puffing rapidly. "It's time! I swear it! Force is called for now sir! When he returns tonight we're going to have the local sheriff awaiting him! Can you save him? Do you wish to reason with him one last time?"

I was saddened by this inevitable turn of fortune for Benito. With reluctance I replied that I would visit the premises prior to the expected return of the giant and make one last effort to convince him of easier ways to exist within this democracy. Hastening the business day, giving last minute reminders of the schedule to Kurdish, CM and Missy, I collected my brief and made my way across the windy street to the lower door, climbed the familiar stairs, opened the unlocked door and sat upon a workman's stool nervously awaiting the fateful reunion.

Soon the landlord arrived followed close at heel by a ruddy officer from the sheriff's department. Our conversation was limited, I have little in common with either of those professions, and was doubly uneasy by the absence of tea, (bless my man CM) and the comfort of biscuits.

The hour grew late. Our impatience seemed to permeate the nearly vacant suite of rooms. Often I found myself glancing out of Kurdish's former jutting window in nervous expectation of the white Plymouth turning up the block. But still no Benito. Where was he? Maybe he vanished. The Sulu Sea. Perth. Cape Horn or Ascension Island. Ten thousand miles he could journey. That barrel chest and aerated body could lengthen out ten, twenty, fifty five feet, and glide through ice-free oceans as freely as migrating pods of whales moving to breeding grounds and trackless waters.

Benito Irving White Coyote did not return. I was alarmed. The landlord showed obvious relief. The deputy said he would be available. I made my way to Benito's desk, now covered loosely with a grey tarpaulin spattered with dried paint. I breathed a sigh of relief as I found intact Benito's map. I spread the crinkly cartography over the tarpaulin and investigated the most current trackings of his travels. The pinpricks made their way from Osterville, Hyannis, South Yarmouth and Dennis Port. Then back to Harwich, Brewster, Chatham and South Orleans. Across to Rock Harbor, North Eastham, and South Wellfleet. Then traversed a trail to Truro and stopped at Highland Light. I then traced the jotted latitudes and longitudes that Benito had hauntingly followed from Hudson Strait, down to the Labrador Sea, south to Newfoundland—I could feel the nausea in my belly, the taste of salt in my mouth—lower now to Halifax, 60 latitude, 40 longitude. The ghostly movements spirited the blue paper and as my fingers glided across the map I felt the unmistakable rupture of the last pinpricks in Benito's chart—Cape Cod. Near Provincetown. Off the height of the Highland Light. The pinpricks had converged. Blue and white pins absent now but with their fateful harpoonings evident. I was giddy. Emotional. There was still light enough to drive up the Cape. I rushed crazily down the stairs to my car, threw my jacket to the seat beside me, and unceremoniously gunned the motor into high gear. The roads in New England turn in many directions as they head but for one, and many a traveler has soon discovered the swiftest way to "Tarwathie" is at moderate speed. I could not readily understand my uncharacteristic haste. On I sped. Past Acushnet. Through Wareham and Buzzard's Bay—a more direct route than that of my former apprentice—along East Sandwich and Barnstable. Out to South Dennis and Long Pond and Orleans and sheltered Eastham. Past the dunes and the troubled road and the town of Truro where lengths away stood the Highland Light. It was quite dark now. The lonely coast absorbed the steady berating of a ceaseless sea. As I emerged from my vehicle there sat his white Plymouth, empty, a shell. I peered into the window where across the hump of the floor leaned, tilted, his cane, black, foreboding, gnarled. And his key. My key once. It dangled from the steering column, still and tarnished.

I climbed the rock to the base of the light, its eye pouring candlepower through the gloom, nothing out there, no ship, no human, no buoy. Nothing. Only the sea and all that the Master put within it. Only that.

Except for the wailing. The low, rumbling wailing. Far away. Out there beyond. Interwoven and pervading through the seam where sea and night and sky are one.

MaaaaaaaSa, MaaaaaaaSa. Don't you know why? MaaaaaaaSa. It moaned that demeaning lyric. That cryptic query. I strained to hear more acurately. Was it possible? MaaaaaaaSa MaaaaaaaSa. Don't you knowwwwww?

Moisture fell from my face and I inhaled gulps of cutting air. Maybe I spoke aloud. I cannot be sure, but the intent of the words tumbled about my head and the sea gathered them up and tossed them over the swell.

I understand Benito. It's not easy to grow accustomed to the ways of the land. To the ways of the people. Nor we to you. It's not easy. So farewell Benito. Farewell. Benito. Farewell.

POSTSCRIPT:

The following item appeared in the morning Bedford Lookout:

ASSOCIATED PRESS — An American whaling ship, The Albatross, was sunk last evening off the coast of Cape Cod, Massachusetts, near the area called Highland Light. Thirteen crew members including its captain perished. Three survivors reported that a great white whale rammed the ship broadsides forcing it into offshore rocks. The Albatross was returning to its home port of New Bedford from a northern quest for the commercial Sperm Whale.

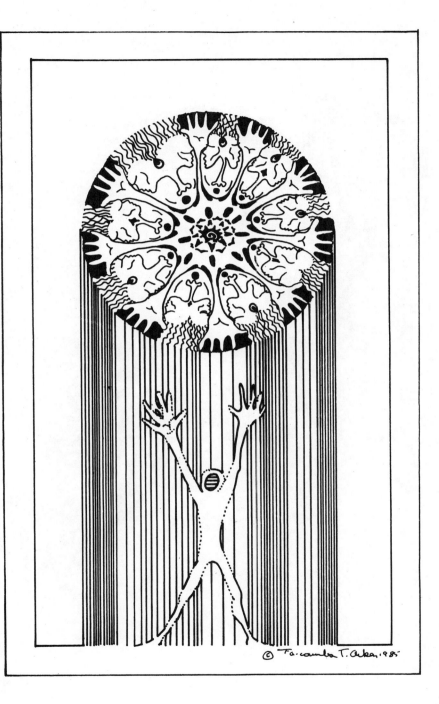

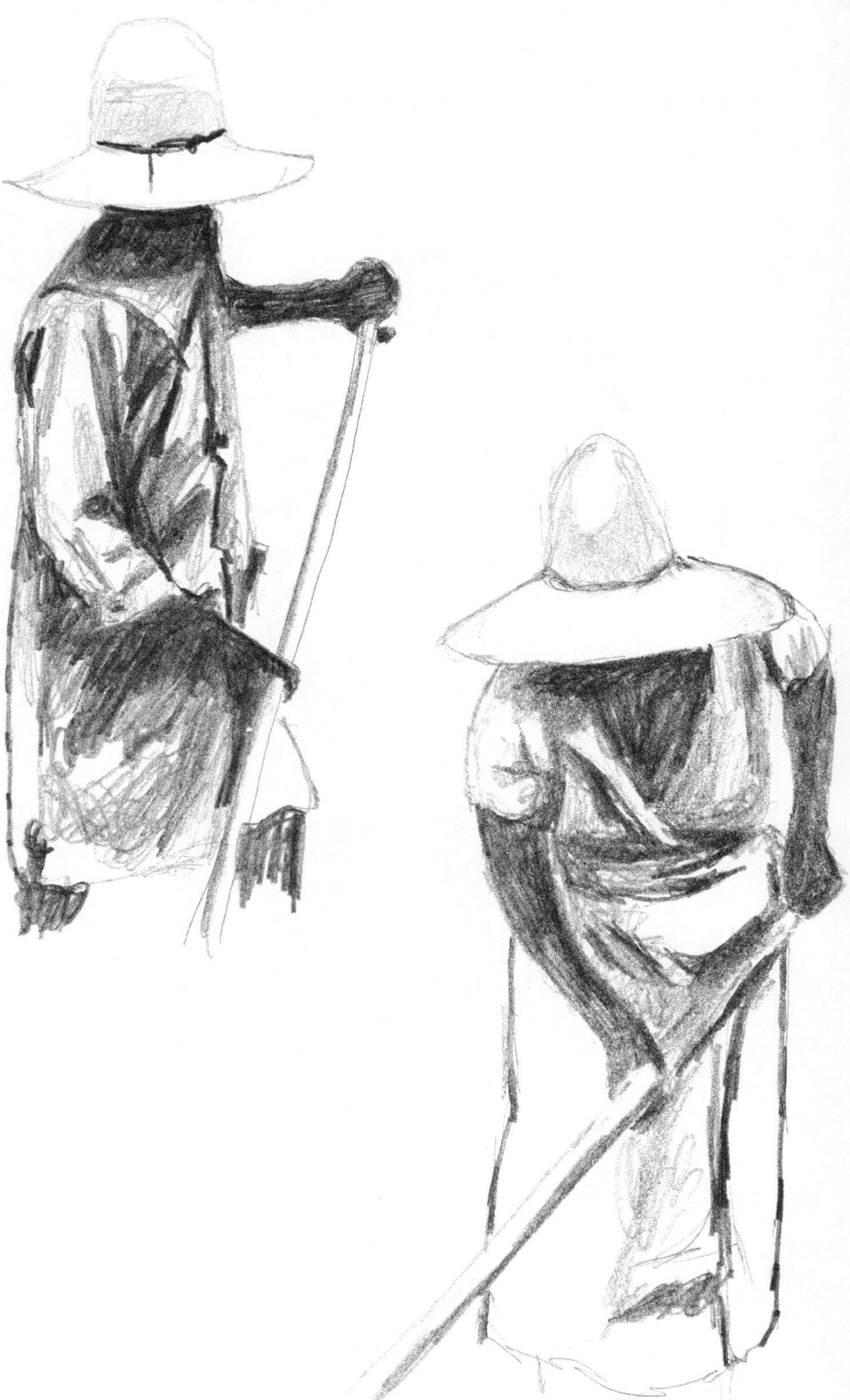

MEDITATION ON MY MOTHER

Louis Daniel Alemayehu

supper simmers as the sun sets over the railroad tracks,
food incense drifts through the house,
bouncin' off the walls and gettin' all up in my head.
all is well
as sweat glistens on Mommas' brow.
quietly Lester leaps in, body and soul from the radio,
                              courtesy of "Daddy-o".
she works over the fire
moving with rhythms and streams in tune with the universe.
                              she loves a man
                              and I understand
                              why *she* is my mother.
fine and mellow, dark madonna
with soulful eyes and kind hands,
                    a giver of life
                    a woman of light,
                    soft and magnetic like the moon
                    through the darkness

                    to show the way
                    she makes a way.

I REMEMBER JEROME

Louis Daniel Alemayehu

I remember Jerome
who came here from Mississippi with his Momma
   in 1953
who was born in July
   of 1945
whose father didn't return from the war, I remember Jerome
the Jerome I met in the school yard
   of gravel and pre-fab buildings
who I told, "I bet I can beat you!"
whose first blow told me, "You a lie!"
Jeromes' first words to me in his southern drawl
   were like some foreign tongue—
   all molasses and defiance.
I wonder now, did he grow to be a man?
Did he escape Viet Nam, dope, cops, "friends", foolish speed, alcohol
   or some other casual dead end turn of fate?
I hope you're alive man
standing strong on this confused land
building and nurturing a future
moving through this dangerous course we now call life
with the wit and quick of a warrior.
I hope you become an ooold man—
in a reasonable number of years.

AFTER WORK

Louis Daniel Alemayehu

On a hot summer night,
at nine o'clock as the sun goes down,
I rush to catch a bus that takes me downtown
where the air is hot and thick and none too good.
I dodge and wait
and sweat and wait.
Transferring to another bus,
I open a window and lean back
hoping to catch some cool breeze,
but it don't work.
Jumping off and quickly stepping down the street
arriving
unlocking the door
rushing up some stairs
unlocking another door and again
rushing up some more stairs
   to find you
          not
       at
        home!

JOE BURSIE

Louis Daniel Alemayehu

Joe Bursie
I like you
cause you a good ole, big ole
    country man.
You been out of the South
    for a good spell,
but the molasses still clings to your words,
    the red clay still sticks to your shoes.
You are an Earth Man,
  Mother Nature's Son,
You are of morning dew, fresh corn
    and pine smoke from the fire,
Rough and rugged over a rose of a heart,
    in this mean ole world.
I love you,
You're my Daddy too.

31 March 1983

NEWS FROM SOWETO: 1976
To Sibalala who "escaped"

Louis Daniel Alemayehu

Automatic gun fire and screams of children.
Like rag dolls they crumple in the road
as clenched fist go limp.
No cotton stuffings here
but rich blood,
external tissue ripped and organs exposed.
Parents return from Jo'berg to the smell
of burning cars and tear gas.
No casual rounds of drinks tonight,
No stupor tonight.
Burnt wall of drinking hall says:
                    "less liquor, better education"

FOR MY BRO — LAWRENCE WILLIAM

Louis Daniel Alemayehu

Do you remember Dinah Washington singing Unforgettable,
          Sunday's fried chicken, mashed potatoes
          with a pool of gravy in the middle and
          succulent green beans, way back
          before black was beautiful?

Do you remember the sweet smell of bananas from Aunt Nellies'
          dining room table, black girls dressed for
          church shining with vaseline in the morning
          sun, Mahalia's sweet thunder form high in the
          choir loft, Dad's steadying hands on your
          first bike and Grampa giving you a silver
          dollar, way back
          before black was beautiful?

Do you remember Rev. Bodie on the radio, Reese and the smooth
          ones on 63rd and Cottage Grove strutting like
          young princes in neon glory, Sugar Ray
          dancing in the ring, the Regal Theatre on Easter
          Sunday, Jackie Wilson on his knees in the spotlight
          crying Lonely Teardrops, B.B. King's pleasurable
          pain talkin' 'bout Sweet Sixteen, Joe Williams
          blowing the blues in front of a Count Basie
          crew and the first time the love light shined
          on you, way back
          before black was beautiful?

Do you remember shirtless summer nights in the projects,
          running hide and seek, the sound of crickets,
          the flash of lightning bugs almost caught,
          the moon, the stars and the endless black sky
          above the railroad tracks and the trees and those
          two story brick buildings we called home,
          way back
          before black was beautiful?

Before we said beautiful was Black,
the beauty of Blackness was before our eyes,
Enriching the deep, deep soil of our lives,
And   we   grew!

CARMEN McRAE

Louis Daniel Alemayehu

Some Creole concoction she,
A gumbo of human spirit she,
Her heart a fine African timepiece,
    powered by Ancestor Energy.
Don't fool around now,
Don't, Fool!
She'll have you walking
    on your eyelashes.
Just might anyway 'cause
When she opens up,
When her voice swells up,
    whirlwind of rhythm and melody,
    can stop on a dime
    and be as quiet as an eye.
    Feather light,
    knife sharp,
    or old wine satisfying and warm.
A weaver of enchantment and charm,
Carmen McRae
    Shines.

FATHER GUIDE ME THROUGH THIS NIGHT

Louis Daniel Alemayehu

Across the autumn sky,
  the wild geese are leaving.
Across the red-orange sunset,
  above the bare arms of trees,
  the warmth is dying in the air,
                                    descending cold
                                    upon the ground.
Twisted fingers
  scratch at the sky,
Abruptly the song of cruel light seems to end
  as the last echo of day wanders off
  and dies in crimson splendor
I breathe in the silence
  and then sigh as bell tones like colors
  drift and diminuendo
  (red, orange, pink, purple, blue, black)
The West lanquishes,
  ruled by women haters
    and profit takers
  while we captives
    dream, struggle
  turn toward the night
    and trudge toward dawn.
With the life-blood of the Death Wishers
fading at my back,
Spirits unknown live in my ears,
  as I sing a song of faith and new beginnings:
                  Soon I will perform my Father's Ritual,
                      solemn, proud and filled with fire,
                  As I sing the sun across the sky,
                  In the morning of my manhood,
                  And some Youth will say:
                                  "This is my Father's House."

SUNDANCER

Louis Daniel Alemayehu

Today
I am rising up
full of youngman fire
and newgreen
moving quickly
moving highly
like sundancer at noon,
my voice has become like swift water
flowing spirit songs
flowing healing songs
for a new world.

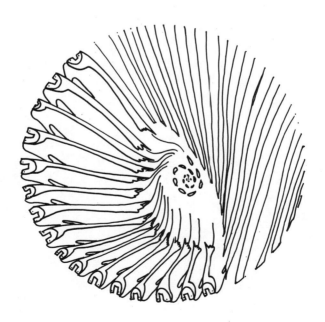

BIOGRAPHICAL
NOTES

Ta-coumba T. Aiken was born in Evanston, Illinois of African, Cherokee, and Irish heritage in 1952. He was educated in Illinois and at the Minneapolis College of Art and Design. He has been a professional artist for many years, with national and international exhibitions and one-man shows. He now resides in St. Paul, Minnesota. He says of his work in *The Butterfly Tree* that "It is a rewarding thing for me to be able to share my African-American experience, hopes, and aspirations with other visionaries and artists who share my heritage."

Louis Daniel Alemayehu was born in Chicago on December 31st, 1945. He has lived in Minnesota since 1964 except for 3 years when he returned to Chicago and worked with poet Don L. Lee's Institute of Positive Education/3rd World Press. In 1981 Alemayehu published his first book of poetry, ANCESTOR ENERGY, and formed a poetry/jazz group by the same name with pianist/composer Carei Thomas and saxophonist David Wright. For Alemayehu, poetry is the spoken/sung physicalized word. The poet sees himself as working in the tradition of "jazz poets" Langston Hughes and Ted Joans, in the spirit of traditional peoples of all colors who *did not* make a distinction between poetry, dance, music and drama. Stirring all these elements together, poetry becomes ritual; its colors — "a rainbow mess," its purpose — healing.

Conrad Balfour is currently an instructor of creative writing at the University of Minnesota. He is the author of a novel, *A Sack full of Sun*, and has another, *The Steerage*, currently under consideration. He is the editor of *The Butterfly Tree*.

George D. Clabon is a native of St. Louis, Missouri. He arrived in the Twin Cities area after attending Carleton College where he majored in psychology. He is currently employed by the Prudential Insurance Company as a supervisor in their policy change area. He has had two poems published in an anthology, "On Being Black," edited by Hazel Clayton, Guild Press, 1982. He has continued to pursue his interest in writing while advancing his career in the corporate structure.

Julie DeCosse says of herself: "I was born and raised in Minneapolis by my mother Virginia. After being educated at Hamline University, I have pursued a career as a mechanical designer. I am married and have a daughter, Rachel. I have been writing since I was ten years of age. My wild imagination and my intense desire to understand reality led me to creative writing. In a world such as we live in today if we had no outlet for our emotions we would surely go crazy. Poetry is my way of not going crazy. My greatest ambition is to become a well-known writer and make writing my profession."

187

Mary Moore Easter makes dances, writes poems, performs both, and teaches dance at Carleton College in Northfield, Minnesota. She toured nationally in her solo concert, MARY EASTER DANCES, with works by Senta Driver, Dianne McIntyre, Irina Lasoff and herself, and she made her New York debut in 1981 with Linda Tarnay and Dancers. Her current work, a dance/theater piece called SOME PEOPLE, is a series of sketches of Black characters revealed through original songs, movement and monologues. She has a B.A. from Sarah Lawrence College and an M.A. in Music for Dancers from Goddard College. Her poetry has appeared in *The Lake Street Review, Sundogs*, and in the collection *Absorb the Colors* by the Northfield Women Poets.

Pamela Fletcher is a native Californian who migrated to Minnesota to attend college. She graduated from Carleton College with a B.A. in Black Studies and from the University of Minnesota with a M.A. in English With An Emphasis in Writing. Her work has appeared in two Guild Press publications, *On Being Black* (1981) and *Survival: Cycle of A Black Woman (1985)*, and in the 1985 spring production of the Whittier Writer's Workshop's (W3) Poetheatre. The 1985 fall issue of *Northern Lit Quarterly* will also include some of her poetry.

Richard F. Gillum has published poems in a number of magazines and anthologies including *Kansas Quarterly*, which awarded him a Seaton Prize in poetry in 1983. His first book of poems will be published soon by Guild Press, Robbinsdale, Minnesota. A former University of Minnesota faculty member, he is now a medical researcher in the Washington, D.C. area.

Donald Govan was born in North Dakota in 1945 and educated in Catholic Indian mission schools. He moved to Minneapolis in 1960 and has lived and written there ever since. His work has been published in anthologies edited by Walter Lowenfels and Clarence Major, and he has one book out, *Fire Circled Rainbow*. His work uniquely combines his Black and Native American heritages.

Soyini Guyton was born in Yankton, South Dakota where she grew up. She moved to the Twin Cities in 1966. She describes herself as a "closet writer." "Whistling Woman" is her first published story.

Carolyn Holbrook-Montgomery is the mother of five and is a writer and actress. She is Founder and Director of the Whittier Writers' Workshop, a Minneapolis based writers' organization that is dedicated to expanding opportunities for area writers by providing programming that is facilitated by highly qualified professionals yet is affordable to people from all backgrounds. Carolyn believes that art belongs to the people and therefore should be accessible to all people.

Seitu Jones is a visual artist who has illustrated books and pamphlets in Minnesota for over ten years. Seitu is a painter and sculptor who has executed many large scale works. His most recent commission is a 250 foot mural for the city of St. Paul.

Essie Caldwell Kammin is a graduate of the University of Minnesota and works as a volunteer advocate at a battered women's shelter. She is a published poet and enjoys sharing her poetry with others, hoping that it touches most in a positive way. Essie is originally from Florida, but enjoys the kaleidoscopic colors of the fall, winter, and spring seasons in Minnesota.

LaNette was born in Cleveland, Ohio. Her poems in *The Butterfly Tree* are dedicated to the memory of her mother.

Jimmy Locust was born in Dayton, Ohio and educated at a small boarding school in Iowa, where he began writing at age 17. He pursued a career in dance in Chicago. As principal dancer and choreographer with Gus Giordano Jazz Dance Chicago, he began to produce his own concerts where he blended his poetry with dance. Since 1984 he has lived in Minneapolis, Minnesota, teaches dance there, and formed the "Final Stage" Dance Company.

Roy Chester McBride. Born 1943; Magnolia, Arkansas. Schools in Arkansas, Louisiana, Michigan. In Twin Cities since 1967. Attended Macalester College. Poems published in many publications. Credits include: SHINDERS TO SHINDERS (A Film), Secret Traffic/Four Poets in Performance (1983 Kudo Award winner), Mother-Child Poetry/Jazz, The Mid-Continent Chorus and Poetry for the People. He is an editor of *Northland Literary Review*, KFAI (90.3 fm) Wednesdays at 7. He is presently working as a creative writing specialist in one of the first private practices of artist/educators in the U.S.

Lynn McWatt is a student at West Virginia State College. She is currently interning at KSTP television, Eyewitness News in St. Paul. She has written poetry for the Summit University Free Press and KFAI Fresh Air Radio in Minneapolis. Her favorite literary influences are Zora Neale Hurston, Alice Walker, Toni Morrison and Ntozoke Shange.

John G. Mentzos began writing poetry at age 9. At age 11, a local press published one of his poems entitled "Minds." While a student at Armstrong Senior High School (Plymouth, Minnesota), Mentzos recieved a scholarship from COMPAS to intern with the distinguished Poet/Author Alvaro Cardona-Hine. Later COMPAS printed a monograph of one of his works, entitled "Beyond the Thirsty Ear." His works have appeared in the book "Seedlings," published by school district 281, and have been featured in the Post newspaper (Minneapolis/West Suburbs), in an article about young poets. He has read his works at the Northside Settlement Coffee House, the 3rd and 4th Annual Black Arts Festivals, St. Paul Landmark Center, the Loft, and at various community events.

Alexs D. Pate is a fiction writer, poet, and playwright whose works have been published widely. He has had two plays produced. The first, *Remember Rondo*, was a winner of the Twin Cities Mayors' Arts Awards, 1984. His second play, *For Children With Missing Fathers*, was produced in St. Paul in 1984. Originally from Philadelphia, Pate was a founding member of the Maj Writers Collective.

Alberta R. Simon is a native of St. Paul, Minnesota and resides in Minneapolis. She is the mother of four. Fascinated by all aspects of communications, she began writing in her early teens and now plans to pursue a degree in Mass Communications. She is currently working on a collection of poems and prose pieces. Of her poems, she says, "The intent was to focus not on the act of rape itself, but rather, the sense of responsibility most women feel in response to a very common, very tragic experience, shared by far too many women."

Marcella Taylor says of herself: "I was born in the Bahamas of African, Native American and Caucasian parentage. I first came to the U.S. to attend college and have lived here ever since. I received a B.A. from the College of St. Benedict (St. Joseph, Minnesota) an M.F.A. from the Writers Workshop at Iowa and a Ph.D. in Modern Letters from the University of Iowa. My first book of poems, THE LOST DAUGHTER, was published this spring by The Renaissance Press, Chicago. I teach Creative Writing, Literature and Film Studies at St. Olaf College and particularly enjoy conducting workshops for practicing writers. I live in Northfield in an old house in town on the Cannon River with a nephew and a cat."